The Cluttering Discombobulator

One man's battle against tidiness, common-sense and boredom.

Written and illustrated by

Paula Harmon

Stop worrying,' said Dad, 'everything will be fine.'

My father Robert

told stories. The less likely the story, the better it was. Life with him, my mother Bella and my sister Jane was unpredictable and fun.

Then I grew up and became sensible.

By the time Dad became ill, I had forgotten where I had put the key to my wild imagination.

But at his bedside, I remembered the years when he could do nothing wrong and I knew that meanwhile, even in his darkest hours, Dad was still making up wild adventures in which he was the hero and my mother forever his beloved heroine

The Text

2012 Monday

London: It is June but it is cold and pouring with rain.

Everything has gone wrong this morning. The country roads to the station were flooded and I would have missed my train, if it hadn't been running behind on its journey from Exeter to Waterloo. Now there are delays on the Central Line. I am going to be late for my course.

The tube is crowded. Workers who normally walk are squashed in damp irritation with tourists and day trippers. I wish I didn't have to stay away for two nights. My wheeled overnight bag is a nuisance. But I feel an unease which is out of proportion to manhandling a suitcase on the underground, wheeling it through puddles in Holborn and being late for a training course.

Dad.

He texted last night. He said 'it was so lovely to see you on Saturday. I feel a bit fluey tonight. Very tired. xxx.'

His texts used to go on and on. Now they are so very brief. I hadn't wanted to check on him too early this morning in case he was sleeping. I wish I wasn't staying away tonight. My house is a long way from my parents, but it is nearer than London.

Security checks to get into the building take ages. I am carrying too many things. It is not until I am finally in the training room that I can put down my sodden case and umbrella and check my phone.

A text from Mum.

Mum never texts. Mum doesn't know how to text.

It says:

'Dad in intensive care. Cardiac arrest. Very ill.'

I find the trainer and say 'I need to go home.'

Home.

Not the home where my husband and children are. Not the childhood home, long sold. But where my parents are. Where my sister Jane will try to be. Home.

Dad - the Adventurer

Moving House

1972 Autumn - I remember…
Despite his favourite pastimes being reading and writing, Dad didn't really like sitting still.

Hard as it was for me to imagine, he had loved horse-riding as a child and had started a cycling club in his youth. By the time he met Mum at seventeen, he was into motorbikes and scooters. They went on hiking holidays in the wilds of Wales and Scotland and then bought a tandem. They got it home via the underground. My modern mind boggled when I heard this, trying to imagine getting it through ticket barriers and down escalators, not to mention squeezed in amongst the other passengers. But Mum pointed out that it was a Sunday and in the early sixties, even London was pretty much empty on a Sunday.

For reasons I never understood, Dad didn't want to stay in the same house either. He worked for the local authority and just kept applying for jobs elsewhere. I am still not entirely clear whether it was boredom or itchy feet. It certainly wasn't ambition. When I was eighteen months old we moved to Bedfordshire, where Jane was born. When I was four, we moved to Berkshire and we moved again within the same county when I was six. We ended up in Wales when I was eight. I sometimes wonder if he hadn't felt we ought to stay put for our secondary education, we might not have ended up in Ireland or crossing the Atlantic.

We had relations all over the place but chiefly in the south-east of England and south-west of Scotland. Driven deep into my subconscious is the belief that weekends are for travelling.

Dad's parents lived in the western suburbs of London in a quiet avenue. My grandfather's semi-professional hobby was portrait photography and the dining room doubled as a studio. The bedroom which had once been my father's was the dark-room. If I was really good I could stand and watch the images appear under the red light. In the kitchen, Granny fed us orange segments dipped in glucose while she baked cakes flavoured with home-made vanilla sugar. The bathroom smelled of Pears soap. My grandmother's bedroom, rosy and feminine, smelled of perfume. In the garden was a tall fir hedge.

'Pull a leaf off gently,' Granny would say, 'now roll it gently between your hands. Now sniff your fingers. It's free scent!'

I was given my first bike there, trundling along the avenue towards the park where the squirrels played.

To get to the tranquility of their neighbourhood, we drove through commercial districts with yellow and red signs and glowing windows. At home in the countryside, shops shut at five-thirty and the town stilled. Families shut themselves in with their TVs. In the outskirts of London, shops seemed to be open all night. We drove back as night fell, passing bright shops selling strange, exotic foods and clothes. The people were different. Women in beautiful saris obscured by thick cardigans walked under pools of yellow street light. We went from the rosy baking-scented glow of my grandparents' house, through the yellows and reds of the shops out into the dark of the road studded only with cats' eyes and headlights. And then we drove home, the town dark but for the soft, obscured light through windows. All those people, thinking they were invisible, played out snatches of their lives in silhouette against the curtains.

Mum's widowed mother lived in Salisbury. We travelled there too, across the Plain, Stonehenge looming in the mist. Granny's flat was on the third floor of a block inhabited only by pensioners. After several hours of sitting in a car, all Jane and I wanted to do was run up and down the landing, but the man below would complain. The flat was peaceful and neat, the blue Tiffany lamp on the oak bookshelf sparkled above the blue dish tempting with mint humbugs. Jane and I would stand on Granny's balcony and look down, our feet between the rails, peering at the geraniums dripping over the edges of all the balconies below, or we'd look across into the back garden of the tall house behind its high wall. We never saw anyone in the garden, or in the windows of the house but they were both well tended. It was as if they were so shy they waited till dark before creeping out: midnight gardeners.

It was in the year after my grandparents left London to live near us in Berkshire, that we moved to Wales.

Dad had applied for jobs in Leek and Mold, neither of which sounded appealing, conjuring up images of a lot of green and possibly slime. He had applied for a job in the Solomon Islands, which he showed us on a globe and looked a long way away.

Then Dad applied for a job in West Glamorgan and got it. He laid out a map on the dining table.

'Here,' he said, pointing to a series of irregular lines labelled in Welsh, 'those are contours. It means that's a mountain. Those lines show you how steep it is. That's its name and it means something like "the range of the wild stallion".'

This sounded exciting. The mountain was very high and most of it was labelled 'Fforest'. The double F made me imagine a deeper, darker place of mystery, filled with elves and wizards. The summit was bare and that, I presumed was where the wild stallion ranged, since otherwise the trees and steepness might get in its way.

At the bottom of the mountain was a river whose name sort of meant 'black water' and after crossing this, you started up another mountain on which the other house would be in a road which meant 'back of the ridge'. I never worked out why it was the back of a ridge rather than just a ridge but perhaps it got lost in translation.

The plan was to rent for a while on one side of the river and then move to the other.

So we upped sticks from our brand new semi-detached house with its double glazing, central heating and view over barley fields and lived for one hot summer in an even newer house which clung onto the edge of a mountain. Its face was a few feet from the edge of the forest and its sloping garden was several feet down some perpendicular steps from the back door.

I remember this move. After a long day, we arrived at night and Dad lifted us out of the car and put us to sleep in our beds in the new house. I recall the packing crates mostly left unpacked, because we weren't staying. It was perhaps the tidiest we had ever been or would ever be again.

I wanted to climb the mountain and find its bare top but was too scared to go further than the first few trees. They soared above me indifferent and the floor was brown with dead pine needles. Beyond that it was dark. If there was a wizard, I feared he wouldn't be friendly. So I spent my time observing water beetles and water-boatmen in the ditch between the house and the forest, still having a vague ambition to be a naturalist one day.

Come the autumn, I started my third new school, and in October we moved into the house on the other side of the valley. A van took the majority of our belongings round by road, but we walked with some things down the steep, narrow path from one village to another. It was easiest to take the cat across the bridge and looking into the sparkling light under the trees and the little sandbank. I knew it would be my place.

The new house was the biggest I'd lived in. It had a view across a field to the bare headed mountain. But the field was scrubby and thistly with a sad horse tethered in a grass-less circle. We had a long, wide garden with bare land to the side. But no-one had modernised the house since about 1960 when they'd put a bathroom in downstairs and built a double garage out the back at the bottom of another perpendicular flight of stairs.

After that glorious summer, the sky settled into a dull, bad-tempered grey.

I missed our old house in England, I missed my old school where I'd finally started to settle, I missed the accent I'd grown up with, I missed seeing my grandparents every weekend. Jane and I shared a bedroom for a while and she complained if the door was shut because it meant she couldn't see the landing light and I complained if it was open, because that way the monsters might get in. I complained about her snoring and she complained I talked to myself. In the end, I got the smaller room where I could kneel up on my bed and look out of my window to the mountain across the valley. It loomed in lumpy darkness.

Shortly after we moved, Dad went away on a training course. He would be gone for three days.

On the second day, the air felt thick. It was almost warm. Our skin crawled and we felt edgy and fidgety.

We went to bed early, Jane and I. She was in the snug corner of her room and I was under the window in mine. I couldn't sleep. I put my light on, spent five minutes trying to memorise my seven times table and then, both failing and bored, started to read instead. After a while, hearing Mum come upstairs, I turned out the light. Knowing she was on the other side of the wall, I fell asleep.

The crash of thunder woke me. I lay there with my heart beating, unfamiliar with my room and disorientated.

Flash. For a second, the half unpacked crate and the pile of books were illuminated and then disappeared. I knelt up on my bed and looked out of the window, counting one, two, three, four... outside was utter night save for the little dots of streetlights and windows in the other village.

Five, six, seven.... Bang!

A pause.

Flash! For a second, our garden and the slope of the field and the trees along the hidden river and the village were all clear. The mountain glowed as if the world behind it was on fire and then they were gone. It was wonderful. I started counting again.

One, two, ... a little sound, my door opening... three, four... Jane climbed into my bed and under my covers, tiny sobs, the sound of a thumb being sucked, Bang! Another explosion, nearer, almost overhead. Jane snuggled closer, her free hand crept into mine.

Flash! Bang!

The world appeared and disappeared, the mountain stood strong, outlined against the beyond and then hid. One, two, three, four, five, six, seven, eight... the storm was moving away.

Mum came in and hugged us both, tucking us back under the covers together. Jane lay in my arms and twiddled my hair. It hurt and I wished she'd go back to her own room, but she was falling asleep.

Then it started to rain. Just a light patter, a few drops, then a little heavier, rattling on the ground below like pebbles being poured into a metal dustbin and then hammering on the tiles above as if trying to drill into the attic.

Mum jumped up and ran out of the room. I dozed and woke to a sound of the slow, steady rumble of incessant rain and something else. Jane, sleeping like a starfish, had pushed me to the edge so that I was held in only by the sheet. I clambered out and went onto the landing. At the top of the stairs sat Mum in her quilted dressing-gown, her head in her hands. Next to her was a saucepan catching drips. From downstairs came a heavy, regular splash.

I had never seen Mum nonplussed before. I sat down and cuddled up. Her face was hidden in her hands and I stroked her dark hair the way she always stroked mine.

'Don't cry Mummy, please don't cry,' I said, 'it'll be all right.'

'I've run out of saucepans and buckets and basins,' she said through her hands. 'That lean-to is like a colander.'

I imagined our leaky house on the waves battling on through the storm and us like Edward Lear's Jumblies *they went to sea in a sieve, they did, in a sieve they went to sea*.

'It'll be all right,' I repeated, 'Daddy will be home tomorrow.'

She made a funny noise but wiped her face and put her arm round me.

'Yes, it'll be all right,' she said, 'is the rain slowing down?'

We listened. It wasn't.

'Come on, back to bed,' said Mum, 'there's nothing we can do and at least there's no carpet in the lean-to. School tomorrow.'

I groaned, remembering, 'We've got a seven times table test soon.'

'What's six times seven?' said Mum, walking me back to my room.

'Is it fifty-four?'

'No idea,' whispered Mum, lifting up sleeping Jane to carry her out.

*****

The rain had settled into a steady impenetrable downpour by morning. Jane and I went to school, leaving mum tipping buckets and muttering things we weren't allowed to say. We got home and discovered her still in the lean-to as if she'd never left. But presumably she had, as she'd found a baby's bath in the attic and put it under the main leak. She was bailing from it and tipping rain water down the sink.

At dinner time, Dad came home. We sat down to cottage pie and he told us all about his course.

'I've been learning about computers,' he said, 'they are bigger than this room but they can work out anything.'

'Do they know the seven times table?'

'They know the million and thirteen times table. But…' he waggled his eyebrows, 'you need to know a secret code.'

This sounded interesting. We sat expectantly, listening to the distant plink plunk of rain dripping into the baby bath.

'You have to imagine one is one but two is one zero and three is one one and four is one zero zero.'

We stared at him.

'It's binary.'

We continued to stare.

'I've got a seven times table test tomorrow,' I told him after a pause.

'Do you? What are six times seven?'

'I don't know.'

'One times seven is…' started Dad.

'The roof's leaking,' Jane interrupted, 'and we had a storm last night and I was very brave.'

I glared at her.

'No you weren't. You got in my bed.'

'Yes and **then** I was very brave.'

'Robert,' said Mum, 'we need to get those leaks fixed. I think there's a tile loose above the landing and there's a massive crack in the join between the roof of the lean-to and the house. Listen to that…'

We listened, the dripping sounded different.

'That means the … wretched bath is nearly full again.'

'Don't worry,' said Dad, helping himself to more cottage pie, 'The rain's nearly stopped and I'll get someone to sort the tile. As for the lean-to leak, it's nothing some duct tape won't fix.'

'I think it's beyond duct tape,' said Mum.

'Nothing is beyond duct tape,' argued Dad, 'and anyway, I have a back-up plan.'

*****

It stopped raining sometime during Friday afternoon when I was busy failing my seven-times table test. By Saturday morning, the last drips were still eking through the crack.

Dad frowned at the baby bath, gazed up at the plastic corrugated roof above and took us all upstairs to the spare bedroom where he flung open the window and peered out. It looked down on the lean-to.

'Ah! I can see the problem,' he said, 'the seal between the house and the roof isn't very good.'

'That's what I've been telling you,' said Mum through clenched teeth.

'You'll never fix *that* with duct tape.'

'It wasn't me who tried.'

'But don't worry, John at work has given me some tar.'

We all waited. Dad pulled his head back in and looked at us in turn.

'What we need,' he said, 'is someone small and light who can stand on the lean-to roof without breaking it and paint tar along the crack.'

We turned to Jane. Jane took her thumb out of her mouth, said, 'no' and put it back in.

I wondered if Dad would pull rank. For a moment, I think he considered it, but I imagine the same image went across all our minds: Jane hanging onto the window sill like a limpet on a rock, wedging her feet against the frame and screaming blue murder. Then, if we managed against all odds to get her onto the roof, refusing to tar the gap, she would paint pictures on the pebble-dash of the house instead. Then she'd paint herself, out of sheer spite. It was too great a risk.

Everyone turned to me.

I went over and peered out of the window. Well someone had to do it.

*****

On Sunday afternoon, I was swinging on the gate when a little girl from a few houses down walked up. I recognised her from school. She was in the year below.

'Hello,' she said, 'you're the English girl aren't you?'

'Yes, I'm Laura.'

'I'm Ffion. My little sister's in the same class as yours.'

'My little sister is a pain.'

'So's mine,' said Ffion, 'and I've got a little brother too. He's even worse.'

She stood for a while and looked up. There was a thick, wobbly, shiny line of black along the join between the lean-to roof and the wall of the house.

Ffion pointed up at the window and then at my hands. I hadn't managed to get all the black off.

'Did you really climb out that window yesterday?'

I nodded.

'My mum saw you. She said "always thought the English were mad. That new girl's climbed out of the window onto that plastic roof and her father's watching from underneath like it's what you do *every* Saturday".'

I tried to rub the black off onto my skirt.

'So what were you doing?' she asked.

'The roof was leaking. Dad said he had a plan if the duct tape didn't work. The plan turned out to be me painting it with tar.'

'Why you?'

'It was sort of fun,' I said, 'apart from climbing out of the window. That was a bit scary. And I wish the line wasn't so wonky,' I wondered how many years I would be looking at my handiwork and wishing I'd tried harder, 'only I couldn't step back and see what I was doing could I? Or I'd have fallen off the roof.'

'What was your Dad doing?'

'Being encouraging.'

'Oh,' Ffion climbed onto the gate next to me, 'they say you've got lots of books and like reading and writing.'

I tensed. I'd only been in the new school for six weeks but had already discovered this was not good.

'Yes,' I said and waited for her to laugh and climb down and go away. But she didn't.

'Have you got a bike?' she said.

'Yes.'

'Fancy cycling up and down pretending they're horses?'

'OK.'

'Then can I see what books you've got?'

'Yes.'

'OK, I'll be back in a minute with my bike.'

She half turned to go and then said, 'your Dad…'

I gulped, 'yes?'

'He sounds like fun.'

'He is,' I said, 'he really is.'

Rain in June

2012 Monday afternoon & evening

Jane is in Leicester with her husband, waiting for her son Charlie to go into theatre for an operation.

Jane's mother-in-law is looking after Charlie's sister Amy at home in Warwickshire.

I ring her.

'Have you heard from Mum?'

She needs to get home from Leicester, leaving the car with her husband and then drive the other car to Swansea. She will have to leave her little boy behind as soon as she knows he's safe.

*****

I am finally on a train heading out of London to Swansea. With flooded lines and delayed trains two hours have passed since the moment I looked at my phone in Holborn.

*****

It is now lunch time and Jane has finally got back to her own place. Her other car is out of fuel.

*****

I get off the train and find a taxi. I ask for the hospital.

'It'll be expensive, love.'

'I know, but my dad's in intensive care.'

'That's a shame. I got problems too. My step-daughter's getting married and she wants her mum at the wedding but me and her mum see, we don't get on like. We don't see eye-to-eye. I don't want her to be there but my stepdaughter wants her there and my husband says not to fuss but I don't like her and she don't like me and I said...'

Shutupshutupshutup I think, but I say 'oh dear, what a shame, that must be difficult.'

It is still raining.

*****

Jane faces a four hour journey to Swansea. It is still raining and she's not sure of the way.

*****

I walk into the hospital entrance with my suitcase and my handbag and my umbrella. Mum is waiting.

'Have a cup of tea,' says Mum, 'he's still unconscious, but he's doing all right.'

'Jane's on her way,' I say, 'she'll be here about nine.'

****

Intensive care is a paradox. There is a sense of utter calm. And yet tension twists your heart.

Nurses walk on soft feet and speak with gentle voices. They lean over patients and talk as if afraid to startle them awake.

Dad appears to be asleep with his eyes open. The skin on his unresponsive hand is soft. There are bruises under his eyes and round the cannula. There are drips. Machines stitch lines of colour to measure breathing and heart rate. They would make a pretty pattern if they represented something else, like embroidery. I am mesmerised by them. The blood pressure drops and a warning light appears. It rises into safety and then drops again. A ventilator breaths for Dad. You never realise how irregular normal breathing is until you hear a ventilator. Normally you breathe shallow then deep, then sigh, then hold your breath, then cough. A ventilator just breathes in and out and in and out in a regular measured rhythm. I breathe along with it and rage against the regimentation. I remember the sound of the inhalation and exhalation from when a friend was in intensive care. But the friend was all right in the end. She was all right. I smooth my father's hand then take photographs in case Jane is too late.

****

Jane arrives at nine. Dad is battling on. We are all together again.

'I feel like I've been on the road forever,' says Jane.

She reaches to stroke Dad's arm and kiss his cheek. He is restless.

'He looks as if he's dreaming,' says Mum, 'I wonder what the dream's about.'

The Test Drive

Robert Darrow felt a little aggrieved. His daughters had accused him of never spoiling Bella and planned to pamper her for her 70th birthday.

'But I do spoil her,' he argued, 'I take her out all the time.'

'Coffee shops, bookshops and church, Dad,' argued Jane, 'nice but not pampering. We're going to give her a day to remember. And then her favourite meal to end the day. What's your favourite Mum?'

'Roast pork,' said Bella.

'No it's not,' argued Robert, 'it's that Vietnamese stir fry I do.'

'I rest my case,' said Laura, 'that's *your* favourite, not hers.'

'You shouldn't interfere,' grumbled Robert, 'and I don't want you bringing her back mutton dressed as lamb or with her hair all sorts of colours. She's grown old gracefully.'

'It's a spa day Dad,' sighed Laura, 'she'll just come back smelling nice and feeling relaxed and I won't let Jane anywhere near her hair.'

Jane, whose hair was a confused mixture of red stripes, grinned. She looked like the Cheshire cat.

'Well at least let me take the children out for the day,' Robert demanded.

All three women looked at each other. 'What, all four of them?' Laura said tentatively, 'you have met them remember. All four of them on your own?'

'I am perfectly capable of entertaining my own grandchildren, even if you think I'm incapable of entertaining my own wife.'

'Same principles apply. They want something a bit more exciting that bookshops, coffee shops and church. Although probably,' Jane paused for diplomacy, 'somewhere sort of where they're trapped and can't do too much damage.'

'I have something in mind already,' he argued, 'you take Mum out and I'll take them out. It'll be instructive, fun and there will be ice-cream.'

Now, a week later, he was not so sure. Laura, always too sensible for her own good, had given him every contact number she could think of in case of emergency and was still fussing as Jane bundled her and Bella into the car. Four children aged between seven and three bounced around him. He had an uncharacteristic urge to bribe his sons-in-law with beer to get them to help out.

But no. He'd be strong - he'd brought up his own children hadn't he? And they'd turned out all right hadn't they? Serious slightly scary Laura and cheerful slightly dippy Jane. A text from Laura came through: 'they have opinions. Just go with the flow. Don't try and argue with them. Especially James.' He didn't remember letting Laura and Jane having opposing opinions. He didn't know what the world was coming to.

He bundled the children into the car and hoped they could all work out the booster seat thing themselves. James sat in the passenger seat and prepared to launch into conversation about some video game. Robert felt they'd have had more fun in the good old days when Laura and Jane as children had been crammed into the back seat without seat belts, little legs sticking to the leather. He put the radio on but James immediately changed channels and some incomprehensible noise issued forth. In the back seat, Ellie and Amy were staring at a shared device and Charlie was fiddling with another. James was still talking video game and hadn't paused for breath. Robert wondered if it might be better to drive the children round and round, periodically stopping at fast food outlets, but no - he had his plan and was going to stick to it. Besides, there was an appointment and he mustn't be late.

The showroom was next door to a burger place and the children all tensed and then slumped, aghast, realising that instead of an array of junk-food, they were faced with a display of accessibility paraphernalia arranged behind plate glass.

'We're going to test drive a new electric scooter!' announced Robert. 'It's state of the art! Isn't that exciting.'

At the showroom, Robert wondered whether buying all those sweets and fizzy pop had been a good idea. James was, at this moment, locked inside the car ostensibly to play on some device but was actually 'investigating'. From time to time, the radio blasted out a different station bouncing between classical and hip-hop at window-vibrating volumes.

The others had come into the showroom with Robert. Amy and Ellie stood on either side like small, sticky bodyguards. They were quite cute, maybe they'd help broker a better deal. Charlie fidgeted on his lap.

'Apart from its all-terrain capabilities, the unique feature of this scooter is that it can turn on a sixpence,' continued the salesman, he paused, 'funny turn of phrase that, "turn on a sixpence", I always wonder what a sixpence is and why you'd want to turn on it.'

Robert opened his mouth to explain, thinking of those tiny silver coins which once had the potential to buy so much and then saw Ellie lean forward to grab a pen and start to scribble on the corner of the salesman's form.

'Wanna wee,' said Charlie.

The salesman paused in the process of finding Ellie some blank paper and glanced from Charlie to the shiny marble floor of the showroom. It would not be improved by a puddle. 'The toilets are back there. Can you er…'

'I'll take him Grandpa,' said Amy.

Robert had forgotten this sort of thing and in any event, not having had sons, it had never been his problem. He wondered what Bella was doing now. Why she'd prefer to be out with Laura and Jane, he couldn't imagine. He didn't approve of huddles of women with their gossip and frivolity. She could have been with him instead, comparing steering mechanisms and gear ratios. Robert and the salesman simultaneously noticed that Ellie had spurned the blank paper and was drawing what appeared to be an angry alien on the upside-down blank contract. Next to it, along the line that said 'purchaser', she'd written in wonky script 'I brd'.

'Is that a little birdie?' asked the salesman in a baby voice, pulling the form towards him as Ellie leant on it. She fixed him with a glare, frowned, then rolled her eyes.

'It's me. I'm bored,' she said. Now that Robert looked at the alien, there was a distinct resemblance between its frown and Ellie's. And perhaps not surprisingly, Laura's.

At that moment, a squeal and crash of doors from the back of the showroom. Amy and a rather damp Charlie came back towards them, stopping to poke all the scooters and wheelchairs on display.

'We couldn't get the tap to work and then it did,' said Amy. Charlie smiled and shrugged and shook water from his tee-shirt onto the marble.

'So, before I decide,' interposed Robert, 'I'd like to take it for a test-drive.'

The salesman indicated the space on the showroom floor, 'there's enough space here,' he said, 'though I might have to get a mop first.'

'No, no,' said Robert, 'I mean in the real world. You say it's all-terrain and can turn on a sixpence. I'd like to try that out. I'll have to use a 5p piece though, it's the closest I've got to a sixpence. Although of course a sixpence was actually worth 2½p.'

'How can sixpence be worth 2½p and anyway how can you have half a p?' said the salesman, then before Robert could answer, hurriedly went on, 'well it's not usual, but I suppose if you sign some sort of indemnity for damage.'

'If it does everything you say it can then it shouldn't get damaged by a few curbs and some grass,' argued Robert.

'It wasn't the terrain which was worrying me,' muttered the salesman, wrenching his form back from Ellie who had drawn a vacant looking man and was writing 'i hat slsmn' next to it.

'Besides,' went on Robert, 'I'll have to leave my scooter behind, I can only get one in the back of the car, what with all the children and everything. You can have it out on display so people can compare and you can work out how much you'll give me in part exchange.'

The salesman eyed up Robert's scooter. Its pockets were stretched and its edges had been chewed by a mouse which had got into the shed where it resided. He glanced round at his display. It would be like putting an old, battered tin can amongst highly polished silverware.

Robert ignored the salesman's expression and got out of the scooter onto his sticks and climbed aboard the new model.

'Come along children,' he said, and made his way to the exit. James clambered out of the car to help with the winch.

'But my indemnity…' said the salesman his hand outstretched.

'You have my scooter and my word is my bond,' said Robert, shaking the salesman's hand and ushering the children back into the car before getting in himself, 'we'll be back in an hour. Or so.'

He pulled off, waving out of the window and James put the radio on again.

The chorus of 'A bat out of hell…' screeched the loudspeakers.

'That man looks worried,' said Amy.

'Nonsense,' said Robert, 'everything will be fine.'

*****

Testing the sixpence theory was fairly easy. Robert drove them down to a car park overlooking the bay near to an ice-cream van. He sent the children to queue for ice-creams and winched the scooter out of the car and onto the pavement. By the time the children had returned with an ice-lolly and four 99s, he had the scooter on the pavement and had dropped a 5p piece to test it on. Charlie climbed back into his lap and they spun in elegant pirouettes. Robert could even do it one handed, as he licked the ice-lolly, although stopping was harder and a sudden jolt sent Charlie face forward into his 99. He turned, ice cream obscuring everything except bewildered eyes. Little bits of flake dropped onto the footplate.

There was the briefest of moments when Robert remembered that one child having hysterics tended to set off all others in the vicinity and tried to remember a calming song. He didn't know any.

'I'll give you ice-cream-o, white glow the noses-o, what is your ice-cream-o, 99 is chocolaty and Charlie's covered in cream-o…' he started and Charlie giggled, a small pink tongue appearing to lick his lips and a rather grubby finger reaching to scrape what he couldn't reach into his mouth.

James, ice-cream devoured, was starting to wander towards the beach. The girls were comparing how far drips had travelled from the bottom of their cornets down their arms and were seeing if they could lick their own elbows. It was time to go.

'Hankies out!' ordered Robert. None of the children had one. All those years of training Laura and Jane had been for nothing.

Robert watched as they did their best to wipe themselves clean with his own handkerchief. He turned down James's offer to help with the winch and wondered how you got chocolate off a car interior. They should go to a nice café and have a quiet sit down and maybe the children would go and wash themselves unaided.

By now, they were bouncing in their restraints and after a short battle with James, Robert managed to turn off the radio and start singing himself. After all, it had worked when his girls were young.

'There once was a boy called Charlie Finnegan
'Got some ice-cream on his chinnegan
'Grandpa's hankie got it off again
'Poor old Charlie Finnegan, begin again...
'There once was a boy called Charlie…'

James and Amy joined in, their voices getting louder and louder. They were ignorant of any sort of tune since Robert was tone deaf and were making up their own. Neither was the same. Nor were either of them approximating Robert's version.

Ellie stuck her fingers in her ears and shouted 'shut up shut up shut up shut up' and Charlie yelled over the din 'my name's not Finneganan...my name's NOT Finneganananan!'

In the rear view mirror, Robert could see Charlie's lip was wobbling. He felt much the same. Perhaps the café wasn't a good idea after all. Maybe he should find somewhere with a stream for the all-terrain off-road test. Now Ellie's lip was wobbling too.

'BE QUIET!!'

He put the radio on to the classical channel and wracked his brains for somewhere to stop, batting James's forays to find pop music.

They drove inland from the coast and up into the farmland. It was high summer. Away from the city and the beach, down a quiet lane, the air was clean and peaceful, filled only with skylarks and distant tractors. He couldn't think of any streams but here at least was a field with a gate open and a broad patch of ground to pull up onto. Robert wished he some sweets and some fizzy drinks to keep the children quiet.

Pulling up on the grass, he let everyone out and deciding that Amy was the least sticky, asked her to help winch the scooter onto the grass. It was pleasant here. He took some photographs and after getting them to wipe their hands on leaves and grass, let the children take some too. In a moment, he'd try out the scooter on the lumpy, grassy ground and then they'd go home. He wondered about getting the children to play hide and seek in the barley so that he could have a little sleep. He gauged the height of the barley against the height of James, who was the tallest. A brief image of his daughters' faces when he told her that he'd lost all four of his grandchildren drifted across his imagination. Perhaps not.

'Selfie!' said Amy.

'Sorry?' said Robert. Charlie and Ellie had climbed onto his lap and were leaning back, thumbs in mouths to doze.

'Selfie!' repeated Amy, 'have you got a selfie stick?'

'A what?'

'It's a stick to take selfies with,' explained James, 'never mind, maybe you're too old for one. I'll hold your phone.'

He grabbed the phone before Robert could do anything and climbed onto the footplate on Robert's right side and Amy climbed onto the back. Leaning forward, James held the phone aloft and yelling 'cheese!' pressed the shutter. Then the phone started to slip from his grasp. Jerking forward to catch it, Robert's body engaged drive and the scooter shot forward through the open gate of the field and into the barley.

Tangled up in the children, he could just about steer but couldn't find the brake. They careered into a sea of gold, crushed beneath their wheels and swaying above their heads. Charlie twisted to get a better view and steered them to the left. All four children were now squirming and leaning, tipping the balance of the scooter and the direction of the steering. Robert no longer had any idea where the gate was. They ploughed on through the barley which parted before them. The uncrushed crop nodded down towards them as if in disapproval. Amy and James shrieked with laughter.

Robert tried to remember which way they'd been facing to start with and work out from the sun's position where they were now. But it was noon. Or more specifically lunch time. The sun was more or less directly above them and so, on a ridge ahead was someone with a pair of binoculars standing by a Land Rover. Or perhaps they were gun sights. No, don't be ridiculous, thought Robert. On the next sweep, he realised he was looking up at the same slope and the person with the binoculars was gone. Robert concentrated. With some effort, he half dislodged James and shook Amy off his shoulders just enough to gain a stronger grip on the steering and his inner compass.

Ah, there was the gate, just down the slope. It was a shame they couldn't get down the same swathe they'd cut on the way up, but there was nothing to be done.

All they needed to do was get through the gate and get the scooter into the car as fast as possible and drive off before the farmer got to them in his Land Rover. And possibly rifle. On the other side of the gate, with superhuman effort, Robert managed to apply the brake and yell at the children to get off.

'Again! Again!' said Ellie and Charlie.

'No, no, quick!' Robert disentangled himself from the children, rescued his walking sticks from James, who was heading back into the field flailing them above his head like samurai swords and unlocked the car. 'Get in! Get in! No Amy, I'll manage the winch, just get in and belt up.'

'Mum says you shouldn't say "belt up",' said Ellie, climbing in after Charlie.

'Your Mum should…' started Robert, but it was too late. A Land Rover pulled up alongside just as James was turning on the radio. A man with binoculars round his neck got out and marched up to them. He stopped, hands on hips and looked from the scooter to Robert and at the children and then pointed at the barley. From the gateway, a flattened path of crushed grain disappeared into the distance. Robert flicked an ear of barley from his jumper.

'Have you seen what you've done to my crops?' said the man.

'I'm very sorry, truly,' said Robert, 'it was purely accidental, you see…'

The farmer suddenly grinned and came over to clap him on the back. Robert rocked slightly under the onslaught and started again, 'no really, I'm very sorry, I didn't mean…'

'Never mind that,' said the farmer and tapped the side of his nose, 'you keep it quiet and I'll keep it quiet. In fact, here's some dosh to say thanks.' He handed over a small roll of banknotes.

'Sorry, what, why?' said Robert.

The farmer took his phone out of his pocket and thrust it in his face. 'Look at that!' he said, 'you've made me a crop circle! I can pretend I've had aliens. I can charge people to come and look. I can get my name in the papers, maybe on the telly. That's if you keep shtum of course.' Looking at the picture, it was true. Somehow, Robert, the children and the mobility scooter had driven a path through the corn which was almost symmetrical.

'Does it look like a Celtic dragon with its tail in its mouth to you?' pondered the farmer.

'No,' said Robert, who was a truthful man.

'Me neither, but we can pretend.' The farmer thumped Robert's shoulder again and helped him with the winch.

'Hiya kids!' he yelled as he guided the mobility scooter into the boot, 'have a burger and fries on me!' and he passed another couple of notes to Robert.

*****

The salesman looked up in relief as they parked up outside the showroom. His face fell when Robert drove the scooter in. Half a field appeared to be caught in it, trapped in wheels and adhering to sticky patches on the footplate and handle bar. Robert got up, brushed a confused beetle from the back of the seat, sat back down and smiled.

'Well I can confirm that everything you've said about this is true. I've given it a thorough testing and it can indeed turn on a sixpence and manage any terrain.'

'But…' started the salesman, 'where have you been?'

Outside in the car, James had the radio blasting 'Magical Mystery Tour'.

'Well off-roading obviously,' said Robert.

'But…'

'So I'll take it. Here's the deposit,' he handed over most of the farmer's cash, 'and you can keep the old one towards it too. What does that leave? About £20? You can take that off my card.'

'But…'

As Robert rummaged in his pocket for his wallet, the salesman looked round to find Ellie drawing on his contract again. The picture was of a complicated incomplete circle with bits entwined around it. One end appeared to be almost like a mouth about to swallow something that looked rather like a human with a tie on. She had written next to it 'drgn eetn slmsmn'.

The salesman gave up and reached for the card machine, 'you don't like vowels much do you?'

30

'Vowels waste pencil,' said Ellie and drew what might have been drops of tears or possibly blood bursting from the human's head. Either way, the salesman felt it was apt.

*****

Robert managed to get himself and the children home with half an hour to spare. Everyone, including Robert, had a new choking hazard toy which had come with a meal from the burger place. Charlie was asleep, Amy was watching a DVD, Ellie was drawing and James was running up and down the hallway pretending to be a dragon.

Bella came in followed by Jane and Laura. They'd made her have something done to her hair, she smelt as if she'd been bathed in perfume and she appeared to be wearing make-up. At any rate, she looked very flushed and was speaking very quickly in a very slightly Scottish accent.

'The beautician was from Ayr,' said Laura in explanation.

'And the person who was serving the prosecco was from Dumfries,' added Jane. 'She's been rediscovering her roots.'

'You've given your mother alcohol!' he admonished.

'You've given the kids junk food,' countered Laura, intercepting James and confiscating a walking stick. She looked at Ellie's drawing. A man was jumping up and down and seemed to be throwing paper in the air. Another man seemed to be crying. And there was a group of four small people and a large plump one on a box with wheels going through a tunnel of trees. Or something. 'Anyway, what did you get up to?'

'Not much. We just had a little drive in the country, didn't we kids?' said Robert. 'I don't know what you girls make so much fuss about. It was a piece of cake looking after them.'

'Great!' said Jane, 'when can you do it again?'

Robert dug around down the back of his neck and pulled out a small head of barley. He went to blow his hands on his handkerchief and found it glued together with chocolatey ice-cream. The sound of James being sick came from the bathroom.

'Never,' he said.

Dad - The Collector

The Birthday Party

1973 - January - I remember

When I'd been little, in the first house I remember, we had had treasures.

'Are they alive?' I'd asked.

The butterflies had danced. They had been very beautiful, iridescent blues and yellows, like slivers of jewels, snatches of dreams, fairy wings.

But they hadn't fluttered. They had floated with wings outstretched, up and down, up and down in stately rhythmic regimentation. Each wing was stiff and smooth, the antennae like needles. When the music stopped, the butterflies in tiers, had also stopped. They had looked like exotic typewriter keys, poised on metal rods.

'I'm afraid not,' Dad had said. We had peered at those long dead insects, frozen in time, imprisoned forever to dance to the limited selection of tunes on a musical box. Perhaps it was as well they were dead because otherwise, doubtless they'd have become sick of the same old tinny ditties played over and over, slowing down as the mechanism wound itself to a stop.

'How are they stuck on?'

'Glue and varnish, I expect,' Dad had said.

I had turned round, knocking into a small pile of books with grey covers and tooled golden patterns, and perused the next thing sitting on a precarious slope.

'What about the squirrel? Is he dead too?'

It had stared at me from behind a glass dome, alert, poised. Its little paws clasped a dusty branch and tiny tufts on its ears looked ready to twitch. A rather disappointing tail was frozen, prepared to flick. It hadn't looked very happy. But then, would you?

I could only have been three years old or so, maybe four. Jane doesn't figure in the memory. Doubtless she had been lurking in a cot or playpen looking solemn and cute, waiting for some visitor to turn up and tell her so. Jane couldn't have done it on purpose at the age of one, but all the same, people never said I looked cute. They said I looked like Dad, which was rather worrying. I would stare at his expansive, cuddly tummy and look down at my tiny one. I would consider his balding crown and check to make sure my mousy hair was still on top of my head where it was supposed to be. I didn't want to wear glasses like he did and I doubted I could make them waggle with my ears like he could. Wonderful as Dad was, I didn't want to think I looked like him.

That had been a few years ago but I remembered the room as if it had been the whole house. Perhaps it *had* been the whole house. We had moved four times since then and I had just turned nine.

'Where's that musical box and squirrel?' I asked Jane. She took her thumb out of her mouth.

'What musical box and squirrel?' she said. She was lining up her dolls on the edge of the piano lid.

Jane scowled, remembering events from our previous house, 'You got in trouble cos of this piano. You told them it was me banging on it. And it wasn't.'

'Serves you right. You used to slam the lid down on my fingers.'

'No I never.' said Jane.

'Yes you did,' I argued, '*and* you cut a hole in my best nightie with the nail scissors. The one with the lambs.'

'Well you were annoying me.'

'Yes, but I was still wearing it.'

'Shouldn't be bossy then,' concluded Jane and put her thumb back in to indicate there was nothing more to be said on the subject.

Trying to argue my case was risky when she was scowling, so I turned back to the music box and squirrel hunt. It was my birthday party later and I needed something to impress the girls from my new school. I was quiet, serious and out of sync. My only redeeming attributes were that I could sort of draw and I liked purple.

At this point, you may be wondering what size mansion we had in which you could lose an Edwardian squirrel in a glass case. The house wasn't that big. Really it wasn't.

It was a fairly standard 1930s semi-detached house. The bathroom was downstairs. We had two living rooms: a small one at the front overlooking the street and a larger one at the back with a view onto the mountain across the valley. We had a small kitchen. The village didn't have mains gas and the house had no central heating. It did, however, have a resident range cooker. Lurking in an alcove, it was in control: capricious and spiteful, one minute cooking too cold, the next too hot. Mum went into daily battle with it, armed with nothing but wooden spoons and spatulas. Generally, the range triumphed. 'You win,' Mum would hiss at it, 'but your days are numbered. Sometime soon, I'll have a new cooker.'

Down the side of the house was a lean-to which extended the kitchen and housed the sink and washing machine. There was another sort of lean-to at the back of the house, in which we had a chest freezer. When it rained (which it did quite a lot) both lean-tos leaked, despite the wonky tar painted along the joins. The house was very dark and pretty cold.

So, you say, *it was dark. But all the same, how can you lose a stuffed squirrel?* Thing was, we could have lost a stuffed elephant.

I did a tour of the place to see what needed to be done to prepare for the party. With my back to the sink, I stepped into the gloom of the kitchen. It really was dark. There was no natural light except for what came from the lean-to windows and no-one had got round to changing the 40w bulb. When we had first viewed the house a few months earlier, its owner was sitting by the range. The range was black, the old lady was dressed in black, the room was pretty black. Since it hadn't been long since Dad had read 'Lord of the Rings' to us, and the old lady muttered with threatening incomprehensibility, she made me think of Shelob in her lair.

Now, as my eyes became accustomed to the gloom, I noticed that most of the work surfaces, as usual, had books and paperwork on them.

I went to the front room. It was full of books. Some of them were still in crates and some of them were on bowed bookshelves and some of them were obscuring paperwork on the sideboard. Squeezed into the middle of the room was the dining table.

I went into the back room. It too was full of books. There was also a sewing machine, the TV, another sort of sideboard with the record player and a reel-to-reel recorder on top, a lot of records and reels of tape. Scattered about were various half-finished bits of writing, sewing and craft projects. There was more paperwork, mostly on the sofa. Some of it was under the cat. There were still a few packing cases, unpacked. The remainder were in the attic, with a massive, abandoned Bible written in Welsh and a skulking dressmaker's dummy.

There was not a room without books or paperwork or just stuff.

It was perfect.

There was always something to read, there was always something to write or draw on. You could put on a record; you could sew something. If you were really bored, you could tear up some newspaper, boil up some flour-and-water paste and make papier mâché. If you were really, really bored, you could make a space in the kitchen and cook something. Only I might just wait until the new cooker arrived.

The thing was, however, that I had a feeling the girls from school wouldn't see it the same way. Karen's house, just up the road, was so immaculate even the dogs sat neatly. Jenny had no books in her house nor did one of the three Susans. Anwen's had about ten books and they were ordered by height. The rest of the bookshelf was taken up with ornaments. Her mother said books were dust collectors. She said it as if dust was a bad thing. Tina had as many books in her house as we did, but they were on shiny shelves, ordered by genre and author. Her house also boasted a fancy bathroom upstairs and a second loo downstairs and they had two cars. The fact that she was horrible and everyone including me was scared of her made it worse that she might find my house wanting. But not inviting her was too big a risk to take.

With Jane trundling behind, I went back into the kitchen where Mum was kicking one of the oven doors and slamming some crispy but un-risen scones on the top. She was muttering some very rude words.

'Mum,' I said, 'can we tidy up a bit for my party?'

'It's not me who makes the mess. You'll have to move anything you don't want upstairs to the spare room,' she said.

'What me?'

'You and Jane.'

Jane took her thumb out for long enough to say, 'Not gonna. It's **her** party.'

'I'd do it for you.'

'No you wouldn't.'

'Little birds in their nests agree,' said Mum proving how little she knew about ornithology.

'Please Mum, will you help?'

Mum sighed and opened another oven and peered at something.

'I hope this cooks and cools in time to be iced.'

I thought of the birthday cake one of the Susans had had. It was shop bought and made to look like an overflowing basket of icing flowers: pink and yellow and purple. It was so sickly, I couldn't eat it and had to bring my slice home for Dad, but it was beautiful. My cake, baked by Mum couldn't compete with that. Hers might taste better, or at least, not as sweet, but it would be iced just plain white with nine candles. I sighed.

'Dad's worked out a design for the icing,' said Mum. 'In fact, he's going to do all your party food.'

Jane goggled sideways at me and her mouth opened, releasing the suction on her thumb with a squelchy plop. I gulped.

'**Dad** has?'

At that moment, the front door slammed open and Dad came in with a load of shopping.

'Don't look so worried Laura!' he said, 'everything will be fine. Your party will be the talk of the school!'

Oh great. Just what I needed.

I'd wondered where he'd been. It was unheard of for him to go shopping without the rest of us.

'It's all a surprise!' he said, as if reading my mind and pushing some brown envelopes onto the floor to make a space for the bags.

'Dad, can you help me tidy the sitting room up?'

'Why? What's wrong with it?'

'There's nowhere for anyone to sit down or dance or anything.'

'Dance?'

'The other girls said they wanted to dance. Like a disco.'

Behind his glasses, Dad blinked.

'I'm not sure I know how to disco dance,' he said. He made a sudden grab for Mum and swung her round the kitchen, stepping on her foot, 'but there's nothing like a good waltz.'

Mum pushed him away and limped into the sitting room.

'Action stations,' she said, 'everything upstairs.'

'I've got reading to do for school,' said Jane.

'You can't read yet,' I said. She shrugged and sloped off.

We spent the next hour taking clutter from the sitting room and putting it in the spare room.

'In the spring, I'm going to move the bathroom up here,' said Dad, piling some half finished drawings onto a pile of books which was wobbling on top of the sewing machine, 'and the old bathroom can be my study. It'll make life a lot easier.'

'Why will it make life easier, Dad?' said Jane, supervising from the doorway with her teddy under her arm and her thumb half out.

'Because then when we tidy up, we can just shove stuff in the study,' said Dad.

While Mum vacuumed the expanse revealed in the sitting room, I remembered about the squirrel and musical box.

'Could be in the loft,' said Dad and pulled down the ladder.

The loft was a world of its own. Things loomed and lurked. Pretty much anything could have been in any of those boxes. I left him to rummage and went downstairs to see what had happened to the cake. It was cooling on the side and for once, it looked as if the oven had produced something edible.

The moment Mum after turned the vacuum off, there was a crunch and yell from upstairs.

'Quick! Quick! Come quick!' shouted Jane from the landing, 'it's Dad!'

'Where! Where!' Mum cried, taking the steps two at a time. We could hear muffled cries, almost whimpers and ran to the bottom of the loft ladder but there was no-one there.

'Come in here!' Jane peered round the door of Mum and Dad's bedroom. She was grinning round her thumb.

The room was full of books and magazines. That much was normal. The bed was covered in dust and bits of plaster. This was *not* normal. Jane pointed up. Above the bed, Dad's legs dangled through the ceiling. His shoes waggled as if he was trying to tread water.

His voice sounded strained, 'stop laughing and come and help, I can't hold on much longer.'

I stood with Jane and watched from beneath as Mum clambered into the loft and helped haul him up. His feet disappeared and a little more dust spiralled down. Above the bed yawned a dark hole. Dad's face suddenly appeared over the edge.

'Come to think of it, maybe I sold them,' he said, 'I definitely sold the musical box.'

A few moments later, he was standing next to us looking at the hole, over which he'd pulled a packing crate, balanced on the joists between which he'd stepped.

'I'll fix it,' he said to Mum, 'it'll be fine.'

*****

After lunch, Dad barricaded himself in front room and banned my entry as he prepared the party food.

Ffion arrived early to help me blow up balloons. She was fairly astonished at the sitting room, which she had never seen so empty and was even more astounded at the hole in my parent's bedroom ceiling. Dad had nailed a thin off-cut of ply-board over it.

'My Mum would have cancelled the party and got the builders in,' she said.

We went back downstairs to check out the record situation. In Ffion's view it was, as I suspected, dire. There were the soundtracks from 'Oliver', 'The Sound of Music' and 'Seven Brides for Seven Brothers'. There was 'The Best of Val Doonican'. There was Beethoven, Bath, Mozart and Brahms.

'Peter and the Wolf' and 'The Carnival of the Animals' apparently weren't going to be any kind of substitute for The Bay City Rollers or David Cassidy.

'Is this it?' she said.

Dad wandered in and blew some dust off the reel-to-reel recorder.

'I've got some Duke Ellington and Louis Armstrong,' he suggested.

'No,' we both said.

'What about "The Goons"? I've got one of their tapes here somewhere.'

'No!' said Mum.

Dad started singing 'I'm walking backwards to Christmas' off-key.

'What are we going to dance to?' asked Ffion.

I shrugged.

'You don't need to dance,' said Dad, 'we're having party games. Pass the Parcel, Musical Statues, Catch the Bunny.'

Ffion raised her eyebrows. Mum was stringing up two flat bits of wood with rabbit faces painted on between two chairs. It was impossible to explain. I wondered if it was too late to cancel the party.

Half an hour later the other girls arrived. Tina peered round making mental notes. There were still books piled up on the piano and several of the pictures were wonky. She looked at the cat and wrinkled her nose as if she was working out whether to sneeze.

We started with Musical Statues. I think that the girls were so startled by having to do it to the voice of Howard Keel singing 'Bless Your Beautiful Hide' that they forgot it was a six year old's game and just enjoyed it. By the time we got to Catch the Bunny (whose rules I never really did understand and still can't explain) everyone was singing along to Val Doonican and laughing.

'And now for the party food!' announced Dad.

My anxiety returned.

We were ushered into the front room and shown an array on the dining table. All the food and drink had been labelled. Chicken wings were 'bat wings'. Sandwiches were 'gravestones'. Sausages on sticks were 'ghouls' fingers'. Cheese and pineapple cubes stuck into half a grapefruit were 'witch teeth'. Silverskin onions on sticks were 'eyeballs'. A jug of cherryade was labelled 'Dracula's Blood' and one of coke was labelled 'Frankenstein's washing up water'. The birthday cake looked as if someone had bled to death over it while a radioactive slug had crawled around and left green slime.

There was a stunned silence. I wondered if anyone would notice if I slipped out and ran away from home so I didn't have to go to school on Monday.

'It's *brilliant*!' said Susan, piling a plate up with bat wings and eyeballs.

'My Mum would *never* let me have this sort of thing!' said Anwen.

Tina sniffed but poured herself some Dracula's Blood.

We all went back into the sitting room and settled down to eat our food to the tones of Julie Andrews singing 'Edelweiss'.

Dad grinned. He wolfed a sandwich and lifted the lid of the piano, idly picked out 'Ode to Joy' which was the only tune he knew how to play. It sounded very odd, even odder than it usually did and not just because it was competing with 'Climb Every Mountain' blasting from the record player.

Dad stopped playing and lifted the piano top. A couple of books slid down the back. He lifted it higher and started to rummage. Two more books fell to the floor. Triumphant, he pulled something out wrapped in newspaper and held it aloft. After a bit of tearing and unwrapping, he revealed a battered, mangled red squirrel with most of the fur missing from its tail. It looked a lot crosser than I remembered.

'Knew I put it somewhere,' said Dad, 'the case had got broken.'

Susan shrieked and then started to laugh.

I looked at her, tense.

'You've had Dracula and Frankenstein and ghouls and witches!' she said, 'this is the Egyptian mummy isn't it? Your Dad is *brilliant*.'

'We'll *never* forget this party,' said Karen, 'we'll be talking about it for *years*.'

And she said it as if that was a *good* thing.

Five S's

2012 Tuesday

I close my eyes and wait to feel awake enough to read. The light from outside floods through the curtains and pierces my eyelids. I know that my back will hurt when I move. I am lying on a £30 Ikea z-bed designed for a child. It was once bounced on by Ellie's best friend. I feel the weight of the duvet with its Disney Princess cover on me and feels bathed in pink with the light colouring the inside of my eyelids. After a while, I hear one of the others go to the bathroom. My body is in a state of mental paralysis and I know when I move it will be to start the day.

I want to pretend that I am in my own bed or my childhood bed, surrounded by my own things; that everything is normal, but I'm not and it isn't. I am lying against the dining table with the head of the z-bed against the sofa. The room is full of books and CDs and DVDs and clutter and ornaments and needlework and craft and photographs (framed and unframed and in packets and on disc) and dust. To put the z-bed up involved a fair amount of floor clearing. The phone is a few feet away, its companion a few inches away from Mum. It is silent.

This is the day when I was supposed to be learning about the 5S's. I know already that there are five and I know they all start with S in both Japanese and English. Beyond that all I know is that they have to do with getting organised, tidying up. Dad's view of this sort of behaviour was that it is at best avoidable and at worse aberrant, not to mention abhorrent. When I have one of my periodic book cull and tidy sessions, Dad reacts as if he thinks his real flesh and blood daughter has been stolen by elves and replaced with a changeling.

I have spent the night half-awake waiting for the hospital to call, but it hasn't. It is too early to ring them. If all is well, if there is still hope, we can go back to sit with him after lunch. Before that, we have hours and hours to fill.

I try to lift myself and my back, curved into the hollow of stretched springs, protests. I roll out onto the floor and pull myself up by the edge of the sofa. I go into the kitchen, put the kettle on then look up the 5S's on the internet. Despite Dad's views on my attempts to keep things tidy, it is not my natural state. His blood runs too thickly in my veins. Keeping on top of housework is like moving sand in a sieve and about as enjoyable. Jane is no different.

All the same, the bungalow is too much for Mum the way it is, even with Dad in hospital. It is hard to get about and hard to clean. There is stuff everywhere. Some of it, in fact a lot of it, is in plastic containers, but it's still stuff. There is no longer a cat to sit on paperwork, so it is held down by other things: photographic equipment, DVDs, books. Jane and I need to do something. Perhaps the 5S's will help.

Seiri, seiton, seiso, seiketsu, and shitsuke

Sort, straighten, shine, standardise, and sustain

I look round and despair. It will take more than a morning, more than a few cardboard boxes. When the kettle boils, I make a pot of tea and start the coffee machine. There is not a lot of room on the worktop. We will start in the kitchen. It will be neat and tidy before the day is out.

When Dad finds out, he'll kill us.

*****

In the afternoon, we sit with Dad, holding his hand and chatting to him. His head turns at the sound of our voices, although it is hard to say if there's a link.

'Come on Dad,' I say, 'wake up. I'm minimalising the bungalow. I need to be stopped!'

'Keep talking,' says the nurse, checking the equipment.

'Perhaps you should put some coffee in that,' says Jane, nodding towards the drip, 'might wake him up.'

'Not the stuff from the hospital café though,' says Mum, 'he's very very particular about his coffee.'

Cumulatorus Confundendum

Ellie was a cat. Ellie was normally a little girl, but at that particular moment, she was a cat. In fact, she was a cat in a basket in the rain on London's Westminster Bridge glaring at Boadicea. Grandpa said it was Grandma's fault. It was all because she'd weeded his books. Ellie wasn't exactly sure how you weeded books, but it was apparently a bad thing to do.

Grandma said it was Grandpa's fault. He shouldn't have gone to the bookshop. And if he insisted on going to the bookshop, he should have thought twice about what he was buying. But she said where he'd *really* gone wrong was agreeing to look after all the grandchildren again.

Everything had been fine until a little over an hour ago.

*****

Auntie Jane had come very early and dropped off Amy and Charlie to play with James and Ellie. Then she and Mum had gone to London for the day.

Grandpa hadn't minded when the kids started playing video games in the front room at seven-thirty. He said it gave him writing time.

'It can't go wrong again' he'd said, 'We'll be fine staying indoors. The kids can run about a bit, I'll show them the book I've bought and we'll watch DVDs and have lots of snacks. And when Laura and Jane came back from London, they can cook us a nice meal.'

Then he and Grandma had a little doze.

That's when it all went wrong.

When Grandpa woke at nine a.m., wondering whether to have a small snack with his coffee, he found himself looking into the angry eyes of a unicorn.

'Er, hello,' he said.

The unicorn narrowed her eyes. Grandpa wiped his glasses and looked more closely.

He said, 'Aren't you usually Amy?'

Ellie wasn't surprised he could recognise her. Amy's fringe was still very curly and her stare was very much like that in a photograph of Auntie Jane as a small girl about to shout 'it's not fair!' and slam a door. Amy couldn't shout, but she could slam a door or maybe puncture it. Or puncture someone else.

Grandma woke up and blinked at the unicorn.

'What's that hissing?' she said.

She turned and spotted Ellie who was on the floor waving a bottle brush tail and then up at Ellie's big brother James, frozen while holding a game handset, apparently carved from marble; then round at Amy's little brother Charlie.

'Sorry Grandpa and Grandma,' said Charlie.

He didn't look very apologetic. He was bouncing up and down, risking serious damage to the spine of an old book which he was holding open in his small hands.

Minuscule bit of tooled russet leather detached themselves and motes of dust flew from the pages. He tried to stroke Amy's mane but she tossed her head and threatened him with her horn.

Ellie stopped hissing to give him a low feline growl and backed herself under the sofa. James did nothing, but then, as he was made of stone, he had no option.

'I don't recognise this book,' said Grandma, taking it from Charlie's hands and flicking through it. She peered at the gilt words on the cover. In ornate script they said 'Magic Spells for the Novice Magician'. She looked at Grandpa and frowned.

'It's your fault,' he said, 'I couldn't find my collection of fantasy novels and then you said you'd sent them to charity even though that was totally unnecessary…'

'Really?' said Grandma, 'there were so many of them, it took me three weeks to pack those books up and sneak them into the doorstep collection bags without your noticing. I cleared almost half a bookcase.'

'Well, I had to replace them, didn't I? So I went to the shop in Lustrous Passage and while I was there, I saw this beauty. I thought it would entertain the kids. I mean,' he took the book from her and started flicking through the pages, 'look at these illustrations!'

Ellie jumped up onto the sofa next to him and looked over his shoulder. Grandpa stopped at a picture of someone in old fashioned clothes flying upside down. It was difficult to tell if he was enjoying it or not. His hat was falling to the ground and people were pointing and possibly laughing or maybe screaming and trying to shoot him down. It was hard to say.

'Anyway, I didn't think the spells would actually work.'

'They do Grandpa, they do!' said Charlie. Amy the unicorn aimed a kick at him.

'Well I'm very impressed at your reading skills,' said Robert carefully, 'but now you need to show me what you did, so I can turn them all back.'

'Oh,' said Charlie in disappointment, 'do we have to?'

They sat down together on the sofa and flicked through the book more carefully. It was a very large, very heavy book. Charlie, it seemed, had turned pages at random looking at the pictures.

'Amy always said she wanted to be a unicorn, I don't know why she's so cross,' he complained.

'I think I heard her say she wanted to *have* a unicorn,' said Bella.

'Oh, well, anyway,' Charlie continued, 'I knew Ellie definitely wanted to be a monkey, but the monkeys looked scary so I turned her into a cat. Cats can still climb really fast. It's not that different really, is it Ellie?'

Ellie glared at him.

'My word,' said Grandpa, 'I never knew cats could roll their eyes.'

'And James was being annoying,' added Charlie, 'it was my turn and he wouldn't give me the handset.'

They all, including Ellie and Amy looked at James. None of them had ever seen him stationary before. It was definitely an improvement.

'Well,' said Grandpa, 'I don't think we can leave them like this, so how do we turn them back?'

'How should *I* know?' said Charlie.

The index was very hard to read. It took Grandpa a long time to find the spells which had already been cast and Ellie began to doubt that Charlie had really been able to read the text. He was two years younger than she was and *she* couldn't read it. Admittedly, she was a cat, and her reading skills had diminished.

All the same, she had a feeling that Charlie had flicked through the pages, found a picture he liked with words he could read phonetically and declaimed them. Finding the unicorn enchantment didn't help. It seemed simple enough to turn someone into one, but not back.

There was no helpful tip box to tell you what to do if you'd made a mistake. Maybe it was at the end of the book? Nothing. Grandpa returned to the start and continued to turn the pages, Charlie gave up kicking James in the stone shins and came to snuggle up to Grandpa while Grandma went to get more coffee.

Amy stretched out on the carpet and looked at her golden hooves. Ellie curled up. James did nothing. But then, what choice did he have? A text came through from Jane: 'everything OK?'

'Charlie's entertaining us. Don't worry,' Grandpa texted back.

Halfway through the book, Grandpa saw a woodcut of a bird. It was a rotund, serious bird with a thoughtful but noble look. He paused. The heading on the page said

To Reverſe Unwanted Enchantments

'It may come to paſs,' he read aloud, 'that thee magician maye wiſhe to upcasſt a ſpell. Hee needeth to wear a taliſman mayde by plaiting three ſprigs of roſemarie with four tail feathers from a male cumulatorus confundendum and thereafter ſprinkled with nutmeg. Hee maye then declaim this incantation…'

'Have you got something stuck in your teeth?' said Charlie.

Grandpa paraphrased it, remembering that the ſ's were, in fact, s's, 'the magician needs to wear a talisman… that's a kind of necklace… made by plaiting three sprigs of rosemary with four tail feathers from a male con… cumulatorus confundendum… and thereafter sprinkling it with nutmeg … what on earth is a cumulatorus confundendum?' He paused, then said 'so Charlie, how do I do an internet search?'

Charlie shrugged. 'James knows.'

'That's not terribly helpful,' said Robert. James was still motionless and solid. Amy was idly prodding his marble back with her horn and Ellie had leapt from the sofa to his head where she now sat in regal elegance flicking her tail.

'I could text Laura,' said Grandma.

'Maybe not just yet,' said Grandpa, fiddling about with his laptop. Emails were fine, writing was fine, photo manipulation was fine but the internet was to him, not so much a web as a mesh. It was worse than when they'd had the Encyclopaedia Britannica.

You'd start off looking up how many feathers there were on moths' feelers and end up reading about Ancient Egyptian knitting, having forgotten where you'd started. Thankfully there were only four entries for 'cumulatorus confundendum'. One was offering to sell a genuine replica on behalf of a careful lady owner for $4000 (without specifying exactly what it was), two were references to references in old books and one…

"'Malloran's Miniature Menagerie, Ineptias Lane, London SW1. Only captive stock of these near extinct ancient creatures. Malloran's has the only known cumulatori confundenda left in Europe. Popularly known as the cluttering discombobulator, this charming bird sheds feathers which were once highly prized by apothecaries since they were believed to contain magic powers for restoring order from chaos.

'*This was no doubt due to the prevalence of the idea that the world could be rebalanced by the use of an opposite, e.g. applying something cold to a fevered brow etc. Cumulatori confundenda live in a state of happy disorder. The cluttering discombobulator mates for life, the male having wooed the female by creating a beautiful nest in much the same way as other birds. However, in the case of the discombobulator, the nest is mainly constructed from an accumulation of largely unnecessary items collected from far and wide (hence 'cluttering').*

'*The female inevitably tries to ascertain if there is sufficient room to incubate a clutch of eggs or indeed simply live. In order to win her, the male distracts her with small items of interest and somewhat discordant singing while surrounding the nest with small flowers until she is mesmerised (hence 'discombobulator').*

'*Despite the fact that the pair spend their life in a state of near bedlam they remain faithful partners for life. Their near extinction is presumed to be the result of the fact that they frequently lose each other in the chaos of their own habitats.*"'

'What does all that mean, Grandpa,' said Charlie.

'It means we need to get to London,' said Grandpa, writing down Malloran's address and phone number, 'before your mother and Auntie Laura find out what's happened.'

'Are you scared of Mummy?'

'A bit. I'm mostly scared of Auntie Laura,' said Grandpa. He sighed and after a bit of fiddling opened another tab on the screen, 'I suppose I'll have to look up trains next but I don't know how we are going to get to London and back in time.'

'Would it be quicker by magic carpet?' said Charlie, pointing at a page in the book.

Grandpa peered at the page and then round the sitting room. The rug was not very big.

'I could probably just about fit myself in the wheelchair on that with you tucked in behind,' he said to Grandma.

'And me! And me!' said Charlie.

'And Charlie on my knee,' Grandpa went on, 'we'd have to leave the er… girls and James behind.'

Ellie jumped down onto his lap and meowed in his face.

'Or, we could put Ellie in the old cat basket and put that on my other knee,' he said.

Ellie growled.

'Basket or stay here,' said Grandpa. Ellie rolled her eyes again.

Amy neighed.

'There really is no room for a unicorn on that rug, plus you don't like heights' he said, 'and we can't move James anyway. Will you be all right looking after him for a bit?'

She whinnied. It was hard to tell if she was smirking but it seemed likely.

'Will James be all right with you looking after him?' Grandpa amended.

She looked to the ceiling and something akin to a whistle came from her.

'Should I put Amy in the garden?' said Grandma, buckling the straps on Ellie's basket, 'only we'll be a while and I'm not sure what unicorn droppings would do to …'

Amy stamped her hoof and scowled.

'Sorry, sorry. Yes of course you can wait. But you might get bored.'

Amy pointed a hoof at the DVD player and used her horn to hook a DVD from its box and put it in the machine.

Only Ellie seemed to notice her sideways look at James.

*****

Half an hour and one hundred miles later, Grandpa made them all visible again and drove off the carpet. He put the cat basket down on the wall. Ellie, her stomach churning, felt herself swaying. Travelling on the rippling carpet as it skimmed the tops of roofs and trees was enough to turn anyone's stomach.

'I never knew cats could turn green,' said Charlie, staring into the basket and withdrawing as Ellie puffed her cheeks out to stop herself from retching. He dragged the carpet out of the wind to roll it up.

Ellie distracted herself by looking round. It wasn't too bad being a cat. No-one made you do anything and you got to stare as much as you liked without being told off.

On the other side of the crossing just at the start of the bridge were three women on a chariot. Their horses looked crosser than Amy and they weren't even unicorns. The woman in the front had her arms above her head as if she was trying to get attention. Bode… bood… bode? Boadicea-Boudicca. That's who she was.

Ellie glared at her. Boadicea seemed like a stuck up old trout. And Ellie didn't know much, but she was pretty sure that in this sort of weather Boadicea needed more clothes on and that putting her arms in the air like that was asking for water down her sleeves.

Boadicea appeared to be stuck at the traffic lights; but then, she was trying to go the wrong way and was surrounded by tourists anyway. Her daughters were leaning out of the back of the chariot trying to see a gap in the traffic but they had no hope. And they hadn't got much on either. No wonder they were all looking grey. And completely frozen. Not even the horses were moving. They must be getting tired standing up on their hind legs with their mouths open. Ellie wondered if they were all dead or had been turned to stone like James.

Ellie was quite proud, in a damp feline irritable sort of way that she even remembered Boadicea-Boudicca's name. As long as no-one asked her how to spell it.

But somewhere in the back of Ellie's tiny cat brain was the realisation that she was confused. But then, she wasn't used to being a cat. An hour ago, she'd been a little girl. And when it all got sorted out, someone was going to be in big trouble. At least, just for once, it wouldn't be Ellie and it wouldn't even be James.

Ellie tried to stand up and banged her head on the top of the basket. *What is it designed for?* thought Ellie, a *gerbil? Mmm gerbil.* Her stomach growled. Then she thought, *Yuk gerbil* and felt queasy again.

She turned her glare on her companions. Charlie was round the corner out of the wind, rolling up Mum's rain drenched, mud spattered rug. *Just as well she hates it already,* thought Ellie.

Grandpa was in his electric wheelchair with his hand on the trigger or whatever it was, itching to be dashing into the crowd. When he got going, he could run over several people's feet in a very short distance. He was getting fidgety because Grandma was trying to unfold some sort of rain cover for him and look at a map at the same time. He was in danger of getting the tourist guide to central London draped over his head while Grandma tried to work a route out on a crumpled cagoule covered with coffee stains. Ellie was pretty sure this wouldn't work. Cats have a good sense of direction, especially when they're usually little girls who have done a bit of orienteering as a cub scout.

There was a cold wind driving the rain horizontally into Ellie's basket as well as flapping Grandma's belongings about in a potentially disastrous manner. If only they'd turn the basket round a bit. She meowed. Grandpa reached up and shifted the basket, dislodging Grandma's arm just as she was about to get the cagoule over his head. But Ellie didn't care. Rain was no longer raining on her. She could ignore her minders, such as they are, and peruse the passers-by instead.

There were not many of them about.

They were mostly in small bare legged family groups clumping splashily under umbrellas chatting in various languages and getting in each other's way as they took selfies.

A few other people wearing smart clothes were rushing, looking at their wrists and shouting into mobiles.

Then suddenly there were two women she recognised.

At first, Ellie's cat brain couldn't immediately remember why right now was not a good time to see them. The women were about fifty metres away, walking together under a struggling umbrella, chatting. One of them was texting, looking at her watch and stepping in a puddle simultaneously. Mum. Ellie remembered. It was Mum. This was the sort of thing Mum did all the time.

Inasmuch as it is possible for a cat to say anything out of the corner of her mouth, Ellie said 'Prrrrp'. Grandpa looked at her and Ellie twitched her ears in a significant manner towards the two women.

Grandpa looked at the women at about the same time as Mum looked at Grandpa, Grandma and Ellie. A slight frown crossed her face and her mouth opened ever so slightly. Grandpa's phone went 'ping'. Mum was too far away to hear it but she looked from Grandpa in his wheelchair to Grandma, completely enveloped in wet cagoule/map to Ellie, in her basket, on the wall.

Mum slowed, grabbing Auntie Jane's arm and Grandpa tried to look aloof by staring up at Boadicea as if he wanted to cross the road and make small talk. Then Big Ben sounded ten o'clock.

Ellie nearly jumped out of her skin and the basket wobbled dangerously on the wall. And at the same time, a taxi went round the corner of the street through a puddle drenching Mum and Auntie Jane up to their ankles. And then they were obscured by an open-top bus driving round the same corner through the same puddle.

Grandpa shouted 'Quick, leg it! Wheel it! Just get on!' as he hauled Grandma and her wrappings onto his lap and Ellie in her basket onto Grandma's lap. Charlie, with the rug under his arm jumped on the back. Grandpa spun his wheelchair and with the engine protesting shot off at five miles an hour along the Embankment.

*****

It was Ellie who found Malloran's Miniature Menagerie. Her sense of smell was heightened and the scent of rodents and small birds was making her hungry and revolted at the same time. She meowed and shoved against the wire front of the basket.

'Stop it Ellie,' said Grandpa, struggling to keep the basket steady and steer the wheelchair at the same time.

'She's pointing with her tail!' said Charlie.

Ineptias Lane had somehow escaped the Great Fire of London, the Blitz and post-war redevelopment. Lost between immense office blocks and off the main tourist routes, it had only three properties on either side and was so narrow that people dwelling opposite each other could almost have passed things to each other across the street from the overhanging top stories of their Tudor buildings.

The rushing office workers barely gave it a second glance. There were no trendy pubs, coffee-houses or sandwich shops down Ineptias Lane, just three possible dwellings, one dusty shop selling bric a brac, another selling old musical instruments and the menagerie.

With some difficulty, Grandpa manoeuvred the wheelchair over the ancient step and through the narrow door which set a bell tinkling. Inside was a table and chairs and a counter, behind which an elderly man wearing a threadbare velvet jacket and peculiar red hat with a black tassel had appeared. Coming from a door behind him was some discordant tweeting.

55

Cagoule and sodden map cast aside, Grandpa put the cat basket on the counter. If the elderly man was startled at the sight of two bedraggled pensioners bearing a cat in a basket accompanied by a dripping small boy carrying a rug, he gave no indication. He simply smiled.

Grandpa raised his hat and said 'Good morning. Mr Malloran, I presume.'

'Indeed I am. Good morning sir,' said Mr Malloran, 'But..' he peered at Ellie over the top of his half-moon glasses, 'I'm afraid I'm not taking animal donations at the moment.'

'Oh no, no,' said Grandpa, 'I'm not donating this cat, she's just come with us because she's my granddaughter.'

'Of course sir, I do understand, one gets very attached…'

Grandma nudged Grandpa.

'Anyway,' Grandpa continued, 'we're very interested in your collection of animals and most specifically your confudatorus… no that's not right, your cumulafundum….your…'

'Utter pink blobulator,' interrupted Charlie.

'Meow!' said Ellie and pushed her paw through the bars of the cage. She just managed to get a claw out and point at the picture of a small bird adorning the front of a brochure on the counter.

'The cluttering discombobulator, cumulatorus confundendum?'

'Yes, that's the one.'

Mr Malloran looked shocked.

'I don't sell them, you know. Especially as cat food.'

Ellie retched again.

'No, no,' said Grandpa. I don't want the bird itself. She doesn't want to eat the bird or indeed any bird. She doesn't even like chicken really. She's pretty much vegetarian.'

'That's not healthy for a cat.'

'She's not a cat, she's a little girl, that's why she's in the basket…'

'We just need a tail-feather,' said Charlie, dragging the spell-book out of the bag on the back of the wheelchair, 'we need a tail-feather to put in tally's mum. Rosemary was in Auntie Laura's garden and Meg was in her kitchen. We just need an utter pink blobulator tail feather and then we won't get into trouble.'

Mr Malloran closed his mouth.

'Tell you what,' he said, 'it's rather quiet today. It's rather quiet most days. You all look rather rain drenched and somewhat agitated. Would you like some coffee or hot chocolate? Yes? Good. Sit you down over there and I'll bring you some. Perhaps you'd like a biscuit too? Good. And then perhaps you can explain what all this is about.'

*****

Half an hour later, under a tree in Green Park, clutching a take-away cappuccino in one hand and the ancient leather covered tome in the other, Grandpa held forth to Ellie, some pigeons and a passing family from Azerbaijan.

Ellie wouldn't have understood what was being said even if she hadn't been a cat.

Neither did Grandma. But at least she knew when to open the basket.

It was less nauseating travelling home by magic carpet as a little girl than as a cat, but not much. They landed outside the house and Grandpa made them all visible again. It was just as well the rain was keeping everyone indoors and no-one was about to see them.

Swaying a little, or in Grandpa's case, steering erratically, they all got off the rug. It was in a sorry state. Muddy, torn at the edges, soaked through. A confused London pigeon which had crossed their path just as they were taking off and had been swept along with them, staggered towards a bush and had a little lie down.

Back inside the house, they found Amy tap dancing on the wooden floor in the hall.

It seemed she'd got bored of watching DVDs and found the Christmas decorations under the stairs. There was no other way that James could have got draped in tinsel and fairy lights from head to foot. Luckily perhaps, she hadn't been able to put the plug into the socket. It was hard to be sure, but Ellie thought his motionless, marble eyes looked crosser than they had earlier.

Grandpa's phone went ping.

'It's your mum,' he said to Ellie, 'her texts are sometimes a little abrupt, but at least she punctuates properly.' He adjusted his glasses, 'let's see, what does it say? "Hi Dad. Having a great time. Home by six. Guess what? This morning saw chap in a wheelchair just like you with someone wrapped in a sheet. And he'd got a cat with him. Did you borrow a cat and get there by magic? Ha ha! Talking of magic, hope kids haven't damaged that old book you brought. Looked like a spell book. Hope James hasn't turned someone into a frog or anything! Ha ha ha!"'

Grandpa turned to Ellie and sighed.

'I don't know what I'm going to tell her about that rug.'

'Never mind the rug,' said Grandma, 'Get the talisman and reverse the spells for these two. I know James can't keep still but I'm sure we'd prefer him not to be permanently made of actual stone.'

Ellie rearranged the tinsel round his head.

'I would,' she said.

'And you can take that book back to the shop in Lustrous Passage too,' said Grandma.

Grandpa looked aghast, clasping the book to his chest.

'No!' said Ellie and Charlie together.

'This has been the best day ever!' said Ellie, 'when can we do it again?'

'Well…' said Grandpa.

'Are you mad?' said Grandma.

'Probably,' said Grandpa, 'but would you have me any other way?

Dad - The Traveller

The Caravan

1973 - Summer - I remember
Dad bought a portable TV and made space for it on the sideboard.
'We can watch television while we're eating dinner,' he
said.
'I thought you said people shouldn't do that,' I pointed out.
'As long as we're not eating off our laps it's all right.'
'Can we start putting our elbows on the table too?' asked
Jane.

'No. Anyway, the thing is,' he said, turning it on and fiddling with the aerial, 'there's a new programme about holidays which comes on at dinner time and I thought it might give us some ideas.'

Jane and I exchanged glances. Was this a good thing or a bad thing? It was hard to say.

Perhaps I should give you some background.

I suppose technically, my first holiday was when my parents went hiking just after Mum found out she was three months pregnant. She carried a heavy rucksack and went camping in the middle of nowhere. I try not to take this personally. She says it kept her mind off morning sickness. Shortly after my birth, there was the trip to Scotland with an aunt in a Fiat 500. Dad always said I ate my carry-cot but I suspect this is an exaggeration.

Then, after Jane was born, he bought a VW camper and took us to a camp-site in the New Forest. I recall running wild in leaves and bracken, peeking at deer dappled under trees.

'Can we capture a pony and take it home Daddy?'

'I don't think it would fit in the camper, darling.'

'Couldn't it follow us?'

'No.'

Jane spent the holiday sitting bolt upright on logs looking cute and smirking through the thumb in her mouth. When she wasn't doing that, she was throwing balls backwards or making sure I didn't get any attention.

Giving up on the pony argument I went exploring. I came back with fallen branches. We'd watched a TV programme where someone carved a beautiful castle out of a lump of wood. In the absence of the necessary skills to do the same, I found some nylon rope, tied the branches together to make a motor bike and rode it around the dell. It came home with us and was the cat's scratching post for years.

A year or so later, sick of fixing the VW, Dad exchanged it for a temperamental car and borrowed a tent from his cousin.

Until I saw the photographs, I'd remembered this holiday as summertime, which tells you everything you need to know about what's important to children. In the photos, Mum, Jane and I are bundled up in winter coats because it's October. We even had cine film to record Jane chucking the ball backwards. She denies this now that the film is lost.

I sometimes suspect that Dad attracted weather. Perhaps his need to travel ever westward was not so much to find Tír na nÓg but to find as much rain as possible and make us stand in it. Towards the end of the holiday, I got caught in a downpour. A lady in one of the caravans called me in to shelter. I sat in the caravan, chatting until the rain eased a little. The lady gave me a little carved wooden squirrel with rather fierce red glass eyes and I wandered back to the tent.

'Oh there you are, we were worried,' said Mum. She helped me into dry things.

'The wind's getting up,' she said to Dad.

'Well, there was something on the radio about a storm,' he said, 'but we've only got one more night and it would be a shame to go home early.'

Mum eyed the sides of the tent which were starting to billow inwards.

'Are you sure?'

'Everything will be fine,' said Dad, 'don't worry.'

We got up early the next day, mostly because it had been impossible to sleep with a howling wind and pouring rain.

'Breakfast first,' said Dad.

'Robert,' argued Mum, the tent being blown down onto her head, 'I can't cook in this! Let's just pack up and go home.'

'We can't drive all the way home without a good breakfast inside us. Anyway, it's just a couple of bits of bacon and some eggs. It won't take you five minutes. Besides, the children are hungry.'

I was staring at the tent. It seemed to be trying to fold itself up with us inside. Outside, the wind screeched round the canvas. Jane's eyes were brimming.

'I don't think they *are* hungry Robert,' argued Mum.

'Nonsense, it's breakfast time, of course they are. I am. Therefore so are you and so are they. You start frying and I'll start packing.'

To the sound of a gale, creaking branches and lashing rain, Mum stood at the camp-stove and cooked bacon and eggs. The gale forced the sides of the tent inches from the frying pan. Before anything caught fire, she dished up and we shovelled it down, while the rain lightened, paused, then turned to…

'Hail?'

Dad bundled up Jane and put her in the car, then he came back for me. Hailstones were crashing down, bouncing off the car, rolling like icy marbles on the ground, stinging our heads and shoulders. Blinded by the storm, he opened the car door, pushed me inside and slammed the door. On my foot. I howled. Jane, fearful of my getting attention, howled louder. Outside the whole world, including our parents, was obliterated in a wall of white. We were abandoned in the car which rattled and rocked in the wind.

Dad's cousin never quite forgave him for all those bent tent-poles. I don't know if she ever realised how close they came to incineration.

Then there was the trip to Scotland. During one five mile stretch including the border, our car's exhaust pipe fell off three times. Maybe the car had some prejudice against the Scots or was frightened of the great aunts. It's more likely that Dad had bought a duff car.

We spent a lot of that trip in dusty lay-bys, bored, looking at Dad's legs sticking out from under the car. His muffled voice informed us that if Duck Tape won't fix something, nothing will. I had believed him right up until the leaking Welsh roof.

*****

So perhaps you can see that now we were hoping for something a bit different. 'Holiday 1973' was an eye-opener.

62

Here were people like us going on holiday to places where it **never** rained, where **nothing** leaked, where you could swim in **warm** water! Ordinary families were going to Spain. They were hiring cottages, called gîtes, in France. Some were even going to Disneyland in America.

We sat open-mouthed, staring at the screen, food going cold on our plates. Was there a holiday for us which didn't involve tents and great aunts? Which involved actual sunshine and foreign food? America was beyond a dream but Spain would be nice and France (even though the gîtes looked a little dilapidated) … now France would be good.

*****

'You bought a caravan,' said Mum, her voice flat.

'It's got four berths and everything,' said Dad, 'it's only a few years old, but I might do up the interior to make it even more modern.'

The sound of rain ker-plunking into a bucket through a new hole which had appeared in the lean-to roof, underlined my mother's unspoken thoughts about his renovation skills.

My sister and I knew better than to interrupt these sorts of conversations. We held hands and jiggled in silent excitement, knocking a pile of unopened brown envelopes off the corner of the sideboard.

Mum lowered her gaze from Dad to the envelopes. He kicked them out of sight.

'It'll be fine,' he said, 'it'll be an investment. We can let it out. Besides, it'll be good for the kids. Fresh air, countryside, wildlife, history and,' he added as an aside to us, 'dragons.'

'Dragons?' I breathed.

'It's right by the beach. There are usually caves. Bound to be dragons.' Jane and I grinned and hugged each other.

'And we can take the cat!' said Dad, 'no more cattery fees.'

I often wonder how my mother's eyes never got worn out from all the rolling.

And so, in August, we went on holiday. To Spain? No. To France? No. But never mind. For once, the sun was shining.

63

By the time we got to the campsite, our senses were on overload. Four hours of trailing through country lanes had made us stiff. Dad's efforts to install a radio meant there was a hole with a lot of dodgy loose wires in the dashboard. We were reduced to making our own entertainment. Dad had sung his way through the entire contents of the Youth Hostellers' Association song book about three times. We joined in to start with and then simply sat back and suffered.

When this entertainment had palled to the extent that Jane and I started fighting on the backseat, Dad tasked us with trying to make a royal body with pub signs. Jane had to make a King and I had to make a Queen. We looked out for King's Arms, Queen's Head, King's Seat etc. I think I was fourteen before I realised there would never be enough pubs named after enough body parts. Or Queens. Still it kept us quiet for a bit. The anticipation made our need for the loo acute and this was not improved by Kally the cat, who liked car trips as long as she didn't have to stay in her basket. She spent her journeys jumping, from time to time, between Dad's shoulders and the back window-shelf via our laps.

The campsite was on a long slow slope on a cliff. Far below, was the beach, with its wide golden beach and caves. A grey stone farmhouse at the edge of the field stood alongside the road which led into the small town, its newer houses clad in pale cement, almost bleached in the summer sun.

Sun. It wasn't raining. It actually wasn't raining. Dad drove up to the summit of the cliff and stopped to unhitch the caravan.

'Look at that view,' he said. 'Right, get Kally back into her basket for a few minutes while we set up.'

Kally, her fur hot, clung to the back window shelf with her claws but between us we unhooked her claws and shut her inside the basket which we put outside on the grass in the shaded side of the car.

Unpeeling ourselves from the back seats, Jane and I clambered out and stretched our legs.

We watched Dad and Mum for a bit. If we stood around too long, there was a risk someone would make us do something. We backed slowly down the slope.

'Want to play?'

There were two children behind us: a girl around my age and a boy around Jane's and looking just as potentially annoying. They were called Tanya and Kevin.

'We could go down the beach if we're allowed,' said Tanya. We weren't.

'Why don't you play cards?' Tanya's mother suggested. Tanya ignored her and suggested badminton. I didn't mind. No-one can play a proper game of badminton on a slope and any inability to actually hit anything can be blamed on the breeze, but Tanya couldn't find the kit.

Dad had finished setting up by now and wanted to settle in the caravan with a cup of tea. Mum asked me to go down to the farm to see about milk and eggs.

'I'll show you,' said Tanya. 'You get them from Mrs Jennings. Her dog's had puppies, maybe she'll let us play with them.'

'Me too,' said Jane. She put her hand in mine and gripped it with an intensity that made my finger tips go white.

'We live in Glamorgan,' I said,

'You don't sound Welsh,' said Tanya, spinning as we went down the hill.

'We're not. Where are you from?'

'Forest of Dean.'

It sounded lovely. At home, there was forest on the mountain opposite to us: dark and eerie, full of enormous pines, the floor ankle deep in dead, brown needles. Then there were woods behind us, which were wonderful. It had deciduous trees to climb, scattered among the bracken on heathland and there were tall, imperious larches and there was a sort of hollow perhaps full of magic. But it had no name though as far as I knew. It was just 'the woods'.

'Forest of Dean' sounded like somewhere full of friendly wizards and pixies. I glanced sideways at Tanya to try and work out if she would understand. You couldn't always tell.

'What's it like?' I asked.

Tanya shrugged, 'it's got trees, rivers, grey houses and sheep.'

'Mountains?'

She shook her head. I was disappointed. It sounded like home only flatter.

'What's the beach like?' I said, changing the subject.

'It's great: loads of sand, lots of rock pools, masses of caves.'

'Are they the sort of caves that look as if they've got dragons in?' I said.

Tanya stopped spinning and frowned, 'dunno. They smell of wee.'

'Laura tells stories to herself in bed when she's going to sleep,' said Jane through her thumb.

Tanya looked at Jane, 'what are they like?'

'They're OK. Daddy tells stories about animals. Laura tells stories about magic.'

'I don't believe in magic,' said Tanya, 'Come on, let's roll down the rest of the slope!'

Mrs Jennings was the farmer's mother and lived in a bungalow near the entrance to the campsite. She asked us in to look at the puppies. They were adorable. Half corgi: ginger and white fluff, smaller than tennis balls. Jane was entranced, taking her thumb out of her mouth as one of them waddled over to her and tried to climb into her lap.

'Want one,' she said.

'Ask your daddy,' said Mrs Jennings, 'you can have him if you like.'

I was mortified. I said thank you, pulling Jane up. We left the bungalow and started up the slope. It was a steep climb.

'You shouldn't ask for things,' I said to Jane.

'I'm going to call him Sandy,' she said, 'he's going to be just mine. He's going to sleep in my bed and I'll take him for walks and everything.'

'No you're not.'

Back at the caravan, Mum was getting dinner ready. It was nicer than camping. We had a proper dining area: two banquettes and a table which would turn into a double bed later. There was a real stove to make our meals and a larder. We could draw and write at the table and play cards. At night, Jane and I would sleep in bunks at the end behind a long orange curtain.

Jane told Dad about Sandy. Kally, curled up on the banquette next to Mum, raised her head and made a low growl. Dad's response was much the same as it had been about a New Forest pony. Jane slumped back and shoved her thumb further into her mouth.

Night fell and Dad lit the gas mantles which ignited with a pop and glowed golden above the orange curtains. He lit a mosquito coil just in case and we watched the spiral burn down, the cold curved tail green slowly devoured by the smouldering red, leaving a trembling end of ash to drop onto the table. He read to us with all the voices from 'Dragon in Danger' where a little girl found a dragon in a cave on a beach and was whisked back in time to a medieval court. We drank Nesquik which we were only allowed on holiday because it disguised the taste of tepid milk. Our eye-lids drooped.

But behind the curtain we couldn't quite drop off. It was hot and the beach waited. We bickered in the darkness. Dad's voice came low, deep and mysterious:

'"It was a dark and stormy night, twelve villainous looking brigands sat round a camp fire. One, their leader, said unto another: 'Antonio! Tell us a story!' so Antonio began…"'

His voice changed, now it was high pitched and warbling:

'"It was a dark and stormy night, twelve villainous looking brigands sat round a camp fire. One, their leader, said unto another: 'Antonio! Tell us a story!' so Antonio began…"'

Again his voice changed. Now it was chirpy, almost Cockney, he spoke faster:

"'It was a dark and stormy night, twelve villainous looking brigands sat round a camp fire. One, their leader, said unto another: 'Antonio! Tell us a story!' so Antonio began…'"

'Oh for goodness sake, Robert, you're driving me mad!' said Mum.

Behind the curtain we giggled. The gas mantles whispered and our parents murmured and we drifted off to sleep.

We spent the next day, after fighting over the variety pack of cereals, on the beach. Tanya had been right about the rock-pools. They were full of shrimps and I was determined to catch enough to eat. The only shrimps I'd ever had were those in Chinese takeaway special fried rice. If I caught some. Dad would give fried rice a go. There was nothing he wouldn't try.

But the shrimps dodged my net and flitted about like Edwardian ladies, straight-backed and dainty, flicking their skirts to keep just ahead of me. All I managed to do was dig up soft sand which filtered through the mesh while the shrimps twitched their antennae, rolled their beady eyes and slipped into crevices.

Tanya had been right about the caves too. They reeked. Every time I ventured into one, I was repelled by the stench of urine. Before I had braced myself to try again, I was called back to where I could be seen. The day rolled on and the sun grew higher. Dad's bald head was the colour of a strawberry and my shoulders and Jane's shoulders were raw.

'I think we'll have a day of touring tomorrow,' said Dad, 'I'm feeling a bit queasy. Do you suppose it's those pickled cockles I ate?'

In the longer grass near the fences, outside the caravans we played badminton with Tanya and Kevin. Or at least, Tanya and I played.

'Mummy said you had to let me win!' wailed Kevin and ran back to his awning. Jane sat down in the grass and talked to a dog which wasn't there.

The next day Tanya and Kevin went home to the Forest of Dean, magical or otherwise. We went sight-seeing. Resting our sunburnt skin against the hot leather seats was torture. I settled on the middle seat where I could lean between our parents.

'You're sitting on Sandy!' shouted Jane.

Startled, Dad slammed on the brakes so that the car behind nearly crashed into us. He reached round and slapped her legs. After that, she leant silent against the back of Mum's seat, tears running down her furious face, twiddling Mum's hair.

On another hill, coarse with grass scorching in the sun, we found a castle. It was ruined but I lay in the shade of tumbled walls and closed my eyes, listening to Dad explain what each room had once been. I could imagine myself there as a medieval princess, be-wimpled and be-gowned in fine cloth, eating with my hands or embroidering a tapestry or listening to minstrels. I imagined getting the guards to pop Jane into the dungeons for a bit, just to teach her.

At the shop, we bought ice cream, traditional vanilla, so firm you could take bites. It was good but not as delicious as the whipped ice-cream from a van which Dad said was like plastic and tasted of nothing.

The church was ancient and peaceful. Inside were stone effigies of long dead nobles and medieval memorials of knights and ladies. Dad paid for us all to do brass rubbings with long strips of paper and chunky wax. Serious faces were revealed, staring out over a thousand years. Their fine hands were clasped in prayer and their long pointed feet rested on sleeping hounds. It was cool in the church, so tempting to lie down on the smooth flagstones but for the names engraved on them, worn away to anonymity. Were there bodies below us? It was too creepy to contemplate.

We emerged into an evening choking with heat. Although the sun was losing its power, the very land was breathing hot.

On the way back, we stopped at Mrs Jennings for some fresh milk. Without a fridge, what we had was no longer fit to drink.

'Hot today,' said Dad.

'It's sweltering,' said Mrs Jennings, 'and not due to change for days.'

'Look Daddy, look!' said Jane, leading us to the puppies. Sandy waddled over to her again and she knelt down to nuzzle him. 'Look Daddy, he wants to be mine. I want him.'

'You can have him if you want,' said Mrs Jennings, 'they're not pure-bred. His mother got out, the little... rascal.'

'We can't,' said Dad, 'we already have a cat and two rabbits.'

We got back in the car and drove back up to the top of the slope.

'You're so embarrassing,' I hissed at Jane. My skin was itching all over. It looked as if hers did too. She squirmed and glared but said nothing.

Back at the top of the slope, Kally came out of the shade underneath the caravan.

'Some people have leads for their cats,' said Dad, 'and take them for walks.' We all looked at Kally. She looked back at us and made a noise which sounded like a snigger. I swear her eyebrow whiskers raised.

'It's not the same,' said Jane, 'cats are stupid.'

'Come on, I'll take your mind off it,' said Dad, 'look what I borrowed from John in the office.'

He rummaged about in the boot and pulled out a bag.

'Inside here,' he said, 'inside here is our dinner!'

We stared at him. The bag had been in the boot for three days.

'Not more tins,' said Jane.

'Aha! No,' he said, 'it's a special rod for sea-fishing. We're going down to the beach and I'll set it up. Within an hour we'll have buckets of mackerel and bream and bass and…we'll have so much, you can sell it round the campsite.'

'Can we keep the money?'

'Well, maybe,' said Dad. He weighed up whether to drive down the slope or walk. It seemed a shame to get back into the stuffy car, but on the other hand, it would be hard to carry all the fish back up the slope later.

Kally stretched out in the evening sun. For a while, she watched the wheeling sea-gulls but then, settling her shoulders as if shrugging, relaxed.

'Prrp,' she said, closing her eyes.

On the beach, there were already other fishermen, their long rods propped up in the sand, the lines stretched out into the rollers. Even with help from another fisherman, it took Dad the best part of the first hour to set up. We sat on the hard, cooling beach and watched. The sun was setting and the sky was turning a smoky pinkish blue. Staring out into the west, we could no longer make out the end of the fishing line in the blurring sea. The rollers rolled and thundered towards us, fizzling out into lacy wavelets on the shore.

After a while, Jane and I got bored of watching the line of near motionless men silhouetted along the shore. Nothing was happening. Dad tweaked and fiddled, but there was no sign of a bite. We got up to explore.

'Don't go too far,' said Mum, sketching the sea and the sun and the fishermen.

We scraped a hopscotch grid in the sand and played for a while, using shells as markers. It was past dinner time and we were hungry. I picked up a shell and threw it, but a slight breeze flew it off the grid.

'That was mine,' said Jane, 'you're cheating. I'm not playing anymore.'

She stomped off back towards the water's edge and dared the waves to touch her toes. Oblivious, they trickled onwards anyway so she dug a moat around her feet and watched it fill and drain.

I wandered off to look at the rock-pools. In the dusk, it was impossible to make out the life in them. The sea-anemones were glistening blobs of red jelly waiting for the tide to turn and bring more food. The shrimps were invisible. I strained my eyes trying to see if there was movement against the sand but I couldn't be sure. I carried on towards the back of the beach where the sand turned to shingle and then large, smooth stones. The caves were there, shallow ones with little interest, and deeper ones, curving away under the cliffs, their ends out of sight. I ventured into one. The stench of stale urine filled my nostrils, but the cave made noises, little sounds seeping out. I stepped a little further, balancing from stone to stone. Behind me the colour was washing out of the beach as the sun set, but there was still some light. Ahead of me the cave was dark and whispering.

'Laura! Laura! He's caught something! Come quick!'

Mum was beckoning. The cave went quiet. I turned and balancing over the stones, I went back onto the beach and breathed again.

Back at the shore, Dad was wrestling with the rod.

'I reckon it's enormous!' he said, 'did I ever tell you that one of your Medieval ancestors caught a whale off London Bridge? It's in the family tree… here it comes….'

He reeled and heaved and the line raced through the water until the end spun up into the air, glittering in the last of the sun and he landed…he landed the smallest flounder anyone had ever seen, the size of Jane's foot but flatter. It twisted and flickered on the sand.

'Humph,' said Dad, 'well we can give that one to Kally.'

He dispatched the flounder and looked at the rod, then at his watch, then at Mum.

'Corned beef and potatoes?' she said.

'Well, at least I tried,' said Dad, watching the rolling waves as he packed up. The other fishermen were still there, patient, waiting for the turning tide to bring them food, just like the anemones, only not as pretty.

Back at the caravan, Kally ate the flounder in three mouthfuls.

'Fishing isn't active enough,' said Dad, 'next year, I'm going to try surfing. What are you all staring at?'

'It's the thought of you in a wetsuit,' said Mum.

There was a cough. We looked down at Kally. She looked at us, then vomited the flounder all over the grass.

'No-one appreciates me,' said Dad.

*****

That night started so hot, I pushed back the blanket on the top bunk and told myself a story about a girl who found a friendly elf living in the house who could take her on adventures which didn't involve parents, sisters, tinned potatoes or slightly off milk. Jane lay on the bunk below, sucking her thumb and twiddling her hair. There was a flat space below her feet where the invisible dog slept. No-one else was allowed to sit there. I drifted off to the whispering of the gas mantles and the murmurings of Dad. A soft breeze rattled the windows.

In my dream, the elf and I found ourselves on a boat. It bobbed for a while and then the waters grew rougher. The boat started to rock, someone was shouting…

'Wake up! Laura, wake up!' Mum touched my shoulder and whispered.

It was pitch dark. Midnight. The caravan was shaking and around us the wind whistled in the windows and under the chassis. Kally was deep under Mum and Dad's bed, growling deep and low.

I sat up and bumped my head on the ceiling. Mum helped me find my foothold on the ladder and get down. I slumped onto Jane's bunk. The invisible dog would just have to lump it. In any event, Jane was sleeping on, oblivious to the howling and the movement.

'Mum & I have to move the caravan down the slope. No point in packing up and towing, we'll do it by hand,' whispered Dad, 'But what we need is for someone to check we're on the flat when we stop. Can you lie on our bed and look at this spirit level? You know how it works don't you? When that bubble is in the middle, everything's OK.'

'Why me?'

'You're the oldest and anyway, we can't wake Jane, look at her, she's fast asleep,' said Mum, 'doesn't she look sweet?'

I rubbed my eyes and peered at my sister. She was sucking her thumb. Her lids flickered open enough for a sliver of brown eyes to catch mine, then close again. The mouth round her thumb smiled. I squirmed on the invisible dog, but the smile just turned into a smirk.

As Mum and Dad went out into the wind to manhandled the van, I lay on their bed and watched the spirit-level. The bubble bounced in the yellow-green fluid, now left, now right. The caravan stumbled and lumped down the slope. Plates clattered in the cupboards, Kally meowed. I slid around the bed as the gradient shifted. Away from the top of the cliff, the wind lessened. The caravan moved more quickly now and I watched the spirit-level bubble as it bounced around from side to side from left to right from right to left from side to…

'You could have stayed awake for a few minutes,' said Dad.

'Come on, back to bed,' said Mum.

I stood on Jane's bunk and then onto the ladder.

'Don't step on Sandy,' said Jane through her thumb, without opening her eyes.

'Don't be nasty, Laura,' said Mum, 'don't step on Jane's pretend dog.'

'It's not pretend,' muttered Jane.

'It is,' I hissed but no-one heard.

As Dad did the final re-levelling and Mum watched the bubble, I closed my eyes and tried to recapture my story. But it had changed. The elf had gone. It was just me alone in the wide world.

*****

A few days later, the holiday was at an end. We woke late.

Kally demanded food but wouldn't eat anything. When Dad suggested he tried a last fishing exercise Kally stopped meowing and hid under the table. Jane took the last mini packet of sugar-puffs from the variety pack.

'Mum,' I said, 'she's left me with rice-crispies. She knows I don't like them.'

'Don't make a fuss, Laura, she's littler than you.'

The milk tasted creamy and sour.

'Come on, eat up,' said Mum as I choked and gagged, 'There's nothing else.'

All the eggs had smashed during the midnight trundle and we hadn't bought any more since. The bread was stale and the bacon smelt odd.

'Never mind the surfing,' Mum said, 'next year, can we have a fridge?'

'We managed all those years without a fridge on holiday,' said Dad, 'and anyway, it's not so hot today.' It was true. The sun kept disappearing behind clouds, which was something of a relief. My skin and Jane's was peeling off in long fascinating strips. I itched all over.

'Can we go to the beach?' I said.

Dad looked out of the window. It wasn't so far away now and the tide was well out.

'All right,' he said, 'we've got to pack up anyway, but keep together and be careful. Don't go in the sea.'

We collected our buckets and spades and started down the path. It wound out of sight of our caravan and rounded into dunes.

'Stop walking on Sandy!' snapped Jane, pushing me sideways.

'There's nothing there!' I said, 'you haven't got a dog and you're never going to get a dog.'

'I hate you,' said Jane, 'you get everything you want.'

'Like what?' I said, 'you get your own way all the time. You're a spoilt brat.'

'No I'm not.'

'Yes you are.'

'I hate you and I'm not going to play with you.' Jane turned south along the beach.

'Good riddance,' I said and walked the other way.

It was great on my own. Not many people were about yet. A few dog walkers were out but that was about it. I glanced round at Jane who had settled on the sand to make a castle with her back to me. The sea was a long way off. I paused, wondering if I should go and talk to her. If Mum and Dad found out that I wasn't taking care of her there would be trouble. But I didn't want to make up. Chances were, she'd just scream and shout and throw things at me. She'd get me into trouble no matter what. I could keep an eye on her from a distance and go exploring without her getting in the way and telling me she was bored.

I went back to the caves. The tide must have been high last night because there was no smell this morning. In the fresh light, the biggest one looked cool and ancient, like the church had. The ceiling was high. Fluted rock reached up to dwarf me and the cave curved away from its entrance deep under the cliff. I clambered in over the smooth round stones at the entrance and called out.

'Hello!'

'Hello!' the cave answered.

I turned to look out. The sea was still a long way off across the flat sand. It was impossible to see Jane now, but I knew she'd still be there, digging with her spade, imagining she was cutting into me. Or maybe she had stopped and was making a sand dog to talk to. I turned back and walked deeper into the cave. The sea had draped sea weed and bits of old rope among the rocks.

Without any sun to dry it, the sand in between was still gritty and wet. Above me the roof of the cave was so high my neck hurt straining to look up. I thought of the book I'd read about the girl in the Greek cave, in a trance, speaking in an ancient language as the sea welled up from underground.

I remembered the dragon in the cave at St Austell, waiting to be found. And then there were the pirates and smugglers, hiding treasure and contraband, bringing them up through tunnels out of sight of the law. All those stories must have had some truth once upon a time. It wasn't impossible that this cave could be a portal to another world, or host a sleeping dragon or hold a casket full of jewels. Maybe no-one had ever tried to look.

I climbed a bit further. It was darker. Ahead of me were boulders, piled up against the back of the cave. Impossible to imagine the force of water which had pushed them so far. Perhaps under them was a mystery waiting to be uncovered. I stood at the edge of the huge stones, looking up at them. The cave whispered. It smelt of the sea, of seaweed, of secrets. I could discern neither welcome nor threat. And yet… I climbed a little further and the pile of rocks loomed. For a second, I saw myself climbing onto a giant's beard, the rest of him buried under the sand, under the cliff. Something clattered, yet I had touched nothing small. I turned but there was no-one and I could not see directly onto the beach anymore, I was too far inside. And I felt the cave chuckle. And I imagined how it must be in here when the tide was high and the sea came crashing against these boulders, piling them higher, burying mysteries. I was cold and the cold was not just the cool of the cave. If there was a dragon, he did not want to be found. If there was a portal, it must be elsewhere.

I started to clamber down and my bare foot slipped. A pain shot through me and I tumbled forward, breaking my fall with sore sunburnt arms on the cool smooth rock.

After a moment, I sat up and touched my left foot. It was not a sprained ankle for once. My big toe was at an angle and hurt worse than anything I could remember. I tried to stand on it but couldn't. I called out, but I was too far inside the cliff and there was no-one on the beach anyway.

Sitting down again, I touched my toe. I couldn't walk on it the way it was. Brushing tears out of my eyes, I tried to feel where the break was and as I fiddled, I felt a click as bones realigned. I could just about stand now.

On hands and knees, I climbed down from the boulders and then limped and staggered to the mouth of the cave. The sunlight blinded and the soft distant sea murmured and the warm sand burned under my right foot as I stood one-legged, balancing. I called out again, wiping my tears away to shout:

'Jane! Jane!'

I looked over to where she'd been but she wasn't there. No six year old girl hunched over a bucket and spade digging with fury. I scanned the beach but among the few distant people, no-one looked like her. I dropped my left foot to the floor and tested my weight on it. The pain made me gasp, though there was no-one to hear. But there was nothing to hold on to, nothing to pick up and use as a crutch. I had no choice but to walk as best I could.

Every step was like a burning needle being driven into my foot but nothing was as bad as the sickness in my stomach. Where had Jane gone? If she'd gone back to tell I was in trouble, but what if it was worse than that?

I made my way slowly to the entrance to the beach and was slipping in the soft dune sand when I saw Dad coming the other way.

'Dad! Dad! Come quick! I've hurt my foot!'

He ran down and balanced me as I lifted my toe to show him.

'What on earth were you doing?' he said. How could I explain?

'Exploring in the cave,' I said, 'it really hurts. I think I've broken it.'

He lifted me in his arms and looked round, 'is Jane all right?'

My heart went cold.

'Isn't she back at the caravan?' I said.

'No, she was with you,' his face was stern, whitening under the sunburn, but carrying me, he hadn't enough breath to say much, 'let's get you to your mother and then I'll search for her.'

'I'm sorry Dad,' I said, 'she wouldn't play with me. She went off on her own.'

'You're the oldest, you're supposed to look after her.'

'But Dad…'

He hurried back to the caravan. The jiggling hurt my toe but I cried without making a noise, uncertain whether I was crying from pain or worry or guilt. Everything was packed. The car stood with its doors open to try and cool its interior. The caravan was hitched up, but its steadies were still down and the door was open. Mum was inside checking everything was put away properly. Kally, was sulking in her basket. Dad put me on the banquette next to her.

'She's done something to her toe,' he said, 'and she's lost her sister. The chap in the camper van over there is a doctor. Can you go and get him while I look for Jane?'

He rushed back to the beach.

I sat on the banquette with my foot up. Mum put a cold wet cloth over it and went out. I tried to stroke Kally through the bars of the cage but she kept her back to me, just as Jane had done. I looked out of the window for Dad until Mum came back with the doctor.

'Dislocated,' he said, 'goodness knows how, but she's almost put it back in place.'

He tweaked and another pain shot through me. I wiped tears away with my hands and stared at the streaks in the dirt.

'Nothing much you can do,' he said, 'just rest it until it heals.'

Mum and I waited.

'You're the oldest…' she started.

'I know but…' I started.

She changed the damp cloth for a fresh one and washed my hands and face. We looked back out of the window and saw Dad, coming up the slope, on his own. He got closer and closer until he stopped by the car.

'And stay there,' we heard him say.

'I hate everyone,' said Jane's voice.

He came into the caravan.

'She's in the back of the car,' he said, 'When did she get there?'

'I've no idea…' Mum went out to see, while I hopped behind her, 'Jane, Daddy's been looking all over for you. How long had you been there?'

'Forever and ever,' said Jane again. She was settled against the back seat with her thumb in her mouth. She had bundled her cardigan up to cuddle and looked ready for a snooze.

'You should have stayed with Laura,' said Mum.

'Laura's too bossy.'

'Yes well, I know, but that's not the point. We didn't know where you were. You could have… Anyway, are you sure you're all right?'

'Yes, I just want to go home.'

Mum sighed, 'well we can get going now. And look: poor Laura's hurt her toe.'

'Huh,' said Jane. She closed her eyes or rather nearly closed them. She scowled at my foot and cuddled her cardigan closer, twiddling a loose bit of wool. I thought she might invent some ailment of her own to move the attention, but she said nothing. My toe throbbed and I felt tears pricking my eyes.

Mum went to shut the caravan and Dad wound up the steadies. Mum put the basket with Kally inside on my lap and closed the door. The cat started to fidget.

Mum and Dad settled in the front seats, put their seat-belts on. Dad started the car. He looked back at us in the rear view mirror, frowned and started the engine.

'I know what'll cheer us up!' he said, 'singing! What shall we start with? I know:

"there once was a man called Michael Finnegan!

"Grew some whiskers on his chinnegan!

"Wind came out and blew them in again!

"Poor old Michael Finnegan, begin again!

"There once was a man called…"'

'Oh not now!' exclaimed Mum, 'can't you at least pick something with more than one verse to start with?'

Dad stopped singing and sighed. We waved goodbye to the campsite and the farm and started homeward down the country lane. Mum turned and told me I could let the cat out. With any luck we'd be nearly home before she was sick. Only…

'Kally's being strange,' I said. It was hard to keep the basket under control and each time the cat twisted, pain went down my leg. I struggled to undo the buckles as Kally strained against the bars and then she shot out, ran onto Jane's lap and hissed. Her fur was bristling, her back curved and her tail stuck up like a bottle brush.

'What's she doing? What's she doing?' said Jane.

Dad slammed the brakes on and I pulled Kally away. She trembled in my arms. Jane's cardigan was covered in orange and white fur.

'What the blue blazes…?' said Dad.

From Jane's lap came a muffled woof and a sudden warm stench filled the air. She lifted the cardigan to reveal Sandy, wagging a minuscule tail and widdling over the car seat.

'Mrs Jennings said he loved me!' said Jane, 'I wanted him! You all hate me! You made me leave him all alone! I need him! He's mine!'

Dad muttered under his breath, 'five miles till I can turn round,' he said, 'five miles.'

'It's Laura's fault!' said Jane, sobbing.

'It certainly is. If she'd been watching you…' said Mum.

'That's not fair!' I said, tears welling up in my eyes too, 'she was making sandcastles. How was I supposed to know she'd steal a puppy!'

'Four miles,' muttered Dad.

'I didn't steal him!' wailed Jane, 'he's mine. Mrs Jennings said I could have him. Big sisters get everything first! I just get leftovers.'

She kicked my toe. I shrieked and Dad slammed on the brakes again. There was a distant tinkle.

'If my plates have broken, you two are in even more trouble,' said Mum.

Kally started interspersing the hisses with retching.

'At last,' said Dad, turning the car and caravan into a lay-by. This held traffic up in three directions. Jane sobbing and hugging Sandy, tried to wipe the worst of the urine off the seat with her cardigan.

Ten minutes later, puppyless, we got back into the stinking car.

'Come on, it's not the end of the world,' said Dad, 'everything will be all right!'

He started the engine and pulled off, singing again:

"'I'll sing you one, O

"Green grow the rushes, O

"What is your one, O?

"One is one and all alone

"And evermore shall be so."

Join in everyone!'

Jane, winding down her window to look back, as if she could see Sandy, started sobbing again and Kelly continued to retch. My toe throbbed and I whimpered.

'Oh I can't wait to get home,' said Mum

"'I'll sing you two, O"' Dad sang over the sobs and whimpers and retching.

"What is your two, O!

"Two, two, the lily-white boys,

"Clothéd all in green, O-ho!

"And one is one and all alone

"And evermore shall be so!"'

Jane's distress had reduced to noisy gulps. Poor Jane, she'd always wanted her own dog.

'I'm sorry about Sandy,' I whispered, 'maybe one day.'

'As soon as I get home,' she said, very low, 'I'm going to run away. I hate all of you.'

'And I hope you've learned your lesson Laura,' said Mum, 'it's your job to keep an eye on Jane and look after her.'

My urge to give Jane, or indeed anyone, a hug dissipated.

'When I get home, I'm going to run away first,' I said.

'You always get to do everything first. It's my turn,' said Jane, kicking my foot till I shrieked again.

'I don't care,' I sobbed, 'I'm still going to run away and I'm going to find a proper family who treat me like a princess.'

'You'll never find anyone like us,' said Dad.

With any luck, I thought.

'Cheer up,' said Dad, ready to start singing again, 'everything's all right. Nothing can go wrong now.'

Kally jumped up on his shoulders and threw up down his neck.

Shafts of Light

2012 Wednesday morning

In the morning we go to the other hospital to collect Dad's things. He'd been there for over a month before the cardiac arrest. Until he is out of danger, the ward needs the bed for someone else. Clearing out the locker isn't too bad: clothes, books, mini laptop. But there is his electric wheelchair at the side of the bed, waiting to go home.

'It'll be a nightmare to push,' says Mum, 'how would we steer it? The control's on that arm rest.'

We all stand and look at it.

'I could drive it,' says Jane, 'we could all do with a laugh.'

She manages to get to the lift without incident. On the ground floor, she speeds up along the corridors and loses control, bouncing off skirting boards and walls, nearly crashing through a door into an office. By the time we are all safely outside, tears of laughter are running down our faces.

It's been three days. The sun is shining outside.

'Come on Dad,' I say in my mind, 'wake up and we'll go for a drive down the Gower. You promised me dragons remember? I'm still waiting.'

Hoarders Underwater

Over the sound of thunder, Viridi shrieks: 'You can't have it!'
Louder than the hammering rain, Rubrum howls: 'It's mine!
Get it back!'
Viridi screams: 'No!'
Rubrum wails: 'Where have you hidden it? Tell me…'
Viridi growls: 'Never! It's mine now!'
And over the cove, above the village, the lighting flashes
and strikes the cliffs on either side and fires break out, flickering
red, flickering green, sparking into the night until dowsed by rain
and the waves crash and churn and the from inside the caves
under the cliffs come echoing wails and shrieks and the villagers
huddling in their shaking cottages, tremble.
*****

Laura and Jane seemed to think that their elderly parents ought to spend the summer sitting around reading travel books. One of Robert and Bella's favourite activities was humiliating their adult daughters, if they happened to be available to embarrass. It never failed to get results. Apart from that, their preferred activity, come rain or shine was taking photographs, even if the wheelchair access was poor.

Then Robert decided to enter a photography competition about speed, it didn't go quite to plan. He lowered himself out of his wheelchair to lie down on the pavement and photographed passing cars from the level of their speeding wheels.

Then he couldn't get back up.

Bella, straining to help him into the chair, explained aloud to concerned pedestrians, that no, he hadn't had some kind of attack. Under her breath, however, she said he might shortly experience one and told him to tackle something less hazardous in future. So for once, he took Laura's advice and started surfing the web.

Three months later he phoned her up.

'Hello Dad…'

Robert told her his news. It took a while, but eventually he had to pause for breath.

Laura's voice sounded strange: 'You're going scuba diving?'

'Why not?' said Robert, 'it's experimental. For wheelchair users.'

'What do you mean, experimental?' Laura said. 'You can't take a wheelchair on a scuba dive!'

'Of course you can.'

'Well ok, maybe *someone* can, but *you* can't. You're seventy-two.'

'Now you're being ageist.'

'No I'm not being ageist, you have a heart condition …'

'Yes but it'll be fine, I've decided to go down in the experimental submersible instead.'

'What do you mean experimental submersible?'

This was going to be a long conversation. There was only one thing which might calm her down.

'You can come too, if you like.'

*****

'Alive, alive, oh

'Alive, alive, oh

'Crying "cockles and mussels, alive, alive, ohhhhhhhh"'

It was just like the old days, only with air conditioning and power steering but without the cat. Robert and Bella Darrow and their two daughters barrelled along the A30 into Cornwall singing at the top of their voices and competing to see how long they could make the final note last and how out of key they could all end up.

The YHA songbook had long been lost or possibly handed surreptitiously to a charity shop by Bella, but Laura had tracked down another one. It was wonderful that the four of them were doing this trip together again. To Robert's disappointment but not his daughters' the husbands and children had been left behind.

'It's a shame you didn't bring them along,' he said.

'My word,' said Jane, 'as if it's not hard enough keeping an eye on you.'

'You don't need to keep an eye on me,' said Robert, affronted, 'I'm quite capable of looking after myself.'

In the rear view mirror, he saw Laura's mouth twitch as she looked out of the side window.

'Don't you remember when I went surfing when you were teenagers?' said Robert. 'That was fun.'

'You didn't go surfing Dad,' said Jane, 'you spent two hours falling off a surf board while we video'd you and froze to death on the shore.'

'Well, this is no different really. There are wetsuits involved, anyway. And water.'

'And freezing to death?'

'You should have brought the kids, they'd have been enthusiastic.'

'The kids are kids and you're seventy-two.'

'You two are just too sensible for your own goods. I don't remember bringing you up to be so serious. Where did I go wrong?'

'Mind you,' said Laura to Jane, 'at least we can keep up with Dad. Can you imagine all the kids shooting off in different directions? I'd spent my time stopping James from "checking" the equipment while Ellie decided to climb a cliff. You'd spend yours trying to stop Charlie talking people to death and working out where Amy was hiding.'

'Your husbands would be there to help,' argued Robert.

Jane snorted.

'They were only prepared to come if they could hire a boat and go off on their own and/or hole up in a pub,' said Laura, 'anyway, we just want to have some fun without them for a change.'

'How can you have fun without your children?'

He glanced in the mirror again and caught his daughters exchange glances and roll their eyes at each other. It remained a mystery to him how grown women behaved nowadays. Take clothes for example. Where was growing old with dignity? Where were the muted colours, cardigans and sensible shoes? Jane with hair a colour unknown to nature except perhaps a piece of cherry wood with a blushing problem, was wearing some sort of outfit consisting of loose floral trousers (or perhaps they were pyjamas) and a bright pink top with a floaty asymmetric hem. He couldn't look at it without longing for some scissors to hack it even. Meanwhile, Laura…

'Was your hair that fair when we last saw you?' he asked. It reminded him of how she'd looked at eight or nine.

Laura shrugged, 'The hairdresser took professional umbrage when I asked her to dye it mousy brown and did this instead.'

'Can't you just let it go grey?' said Robert.

'No.'

'And aren't you too old to be showing your knees?'

She was wearing a dress with a turquoise and blue pattern on it which might have been teapots or might have been elephants. He couldn't quite make it out. Over it she wore a lacy purple cardigan so flimsy it was next to pointless.

'"White Stuff" or "Fat Face"?' said Jane.

'Can't remember, not sure if it's either,' said Laura.

Robert wondered what why they had to talk in code too.

The road curved round more hedges and then straightened. Ahead of them cliffs gave way for a harbour with a small village trickling down towards it.

'I can see the sea!' said Jane.

'I saw it first!' said Laura.

'No you never!'

They prodded each other in the back seat.

'That's better,' he said, 'just like old times.'

By the time they had come off the A30 and arrived at the small village of Porthrago it was late afternoon.

There was no-one around and there were no signposts for the complex. Robert stopped to read his directions. Laura and Jane got out and stretched.

'It's very quiet,' said Laura, 'where is everyone?'

The village didn't have the feeling of abandonment. It was simply as if by sheer coincidence everyone had decided to go inside at the same time and stayed there. The closed blinds of the store flickered as if someone was watching and its sign flipped from 'open' to 'closed'. A man appeared in the window of the pub. He shook his head and withdrew. The door was bolted and the specials board blank.

Out of the corner of her eye, Laura saw some greyish creature, a cat presumably, emerge from a half open gate, stop at the sight of them, then slink across the road, its tail waving. It seemed to be zig-zagging, which was odd, but by the time she turned, it had slipped over another wall and out of sight.

*****

Viridi hisses: 'it's no good sending one of the children to the village, they don't know anything.'
Rubrum snaps: 'the children or the villagers?'
Viridi snarls: 'either, neither, both.'

Rubrum whispers: 'then let's see what the newcomers can do.'
Viridi snorts: 'huh! Old people.'
Rubrum mutters: 'we're old.'
Viridi growls: 'there you go again.'
Rubrum murmurs: 'we are old. We're just not…'
And the waves roll into the caves and swirl up the high fluted walls.

*****

Robert swung the car through the gate and into the courtyard. Goodness knows what the girls were wittering about in the back seat. It had looked like a perfectly peaceful little village to him. Hopefully they could buy food at the complex and everything would be fine. As long as it wasn't Jane cooking it would be all right. There is a limit to how much tuna pasta bake even Robert could eat.

The complex was on a level piece of land with buildings round a wide tarmacked area. Racks in the yard held canoes. Wetsuits and diving equipment could be seen through the open doorway of a store, outside which two tanned young men in shorts were chatting.

'Mmm,' said Jane from the back of the car.

'Are you thinking what I'm thinking?' said Robert.

'That they must be cold without shirts?' said Bella.

'Exactly. And how can they wear sandals without socks?' said Robert.

'And don't they both need haircuts?'

'Is that what you meant Jane?' said Laura, smirking.

'Of course.'

'Not idly wishing you were twenty years younger and single?'

'Of course not.'

Robert parked up and got out of the car to walk over to the young men. He saw now the ramp down to the beach, the gradient just right for a wheelchair and a good handrail. Below, agitated waves rolled into caves on either side and were then spat back out. A few drops of rain spattered onto his head. Out at sea, a cavalry of white horses massed, racing to the shore.

'Afternoon,' he said to the young men. They seemed oblivious to the weather, standing there bare chested and smiling. One was sipping coffee and the other stopped rolling rope to hold out a hand.

'Robert Darrow? Pleased to meet you. I'm Ed. This is Kyle.'

'How do you do?'

'Don't worry about the weather, it'll have cleared by tomorrow morning. Just needs to get something out of its system I guess.'

The rain was getting heavier and glistened in Ed's curls and splashed into Kyle's coffee. Neither seemed to care.

'We've got a briefing at seven in the clubhouse which should give you all time to get settled. Your cottage is just down that lane. Is that OK? Have you got everything you need?'

Laura had come out of the car and joined them.

'Hi,' she said, 'is there a shop near here? The village seemed to be on early closing or something.'

Kyle drained his coffee and gestured towards the clubhouse.

'We've got everything you should need in there and the bar meals are reasonable if you don't want to cook. The villagers…' he rubbed his hand across his chin, 'seem to be having some sort of … communal crisis. My gran comes from here, always said stormy weather in the cove made them all go odder than normal. Something like that anyway.'

*****

The cottage was lovely. Three bedrooms under low eaves made Laura think of 'Anne of Green Gables' although the rain was now hammering down and the room was dark and shadowy. Through its window, she could see down to the cove where the sea crashed onto the shore as if trying to batter its way inland. At least she didn't have to share with Jane. That had never, ever worked out.

Back at the complex, with rain battering the roof, they ate bar meals and listened to the briefing. Jane emptied the last of the wine into Laura's glass. Robert took copious notes in the tiny capitals no-one, sometimes even Robert himself, could ever read afterwards. It all sounded very involved.

'You did check with your doctor it was OK to do this, didn't you Dad?' said Laura.

'It'll be fine. Don't worry,' said Robert.

*****

Rubrum cajoles: 'I'm sorry, I didn't mean it.'

Viridi snorts: 'I'm still not telling you.'

Rubrum says: 'I love the way the sea brings out your eyes.'

Viridi growls: 'you can pack that in. My mother warned me about you. "You can't trust them," she said, "they're too good with words, those ones from over the water," she said, "they can talk you into anything." And she was right.'

Rubrum sighs: 'remember when we were young… younger? Remember when we swam together, lithe as fish? Remember when we rolled in …'

Viridi says: 'You can stop the sweet-talking Rubrum. I'm not telling you and that's flat.'

But in the warm darkness she smiles a little, listening to the waves settle into a gentle rhythm and as she closes her eyes, golden memories seep into her dreams.

*****

Overnight, the weather changed. By morning, the sea had had a change of personality, trickling onto the little beach with lacy skirts as if sorry to be dampening the sand.

The sky was a bright clear blue and birds soared. After breakfast they made their way back to the complex where Laura and Jane sat on the harbour wall and wondered why their parents couldn't have taken up water colours instead.

Robert felt a little indecent in the wetsuit. Things had changed since he wore one in the 1980s. Instead of sensible, plain and somewhat saggy black, he was wearing skin-tight grey and day-glo pink neoprene with a mainly pink hat over his bald head. It all emphasised unspeakable things he felt best left unimagined. At least the surf shoes were a sensible grey. Bella looked good in anything, but even he struggled to think that skin tight black and blue neoprene made the best of her figure. It didn't seem fair that she got to wear blue and he had pink, but it seemed pointless arguing. Kyle was wearing red shorts with orange flowers on and Ed had his curls controlled by some sort of Alice band. Robert wasn't sure they'd understand what the issue was.

He had a moment of disquiet when he saw the submersible. It had seemed such a good idea when he filled out the application form in the comfort of the bungalow. Now he thought it looked rather small for three people, one of them himself (who frequently got stuck in an armchair) and one of them six foot Ed (who looked as if he would have to fold himself in half). It was a relief that Kyle was staying ashore.

'Don't worry,' said Ed, pouring himself into an orange and black wetsuit of his own, 'you'll soon get the hang of it.'

'I'm not even very fond of lifts,' said Robert.

'Yes but this has perspex all round it, you'll feel as if you're in a bubble. You won't believe how lovely it is down there.'

'Won't the bad weather have stirred all the sand up too much?' asked Bella.

'Yesterday's weather was nothing,' said Ed, 'but we had a really weird storm a few days ago. It'll be interesting to see what the seabed looks like now.'

'That rough?'

'Yes,' said Kyle, coming up from checking the submersible, 'thunder like cannon fire, a screaming wind and you should have seen the lightning! It wasn't just white but red and green too. It was after that the village sort of shut up shop.'

'Really?' said Bella.

'They told us it wasn't safe round here and to go away, but we had the seismologists and whatnot out and there was nothing to show anything to worry about. Anyway, I expect the village will pull itself together back before the tourist season gets properly underway.'

'Come on then,' said Ed, 'time to get on board.'

Robert waved to Laura and Jane as Ed closed the hatch. Really, for someone who dressed like children, the girls could look very serious sometimes. It must be the Scottish side.

'Your daughters seem very protective,' said Ed, as the submersible dropped under the surface of the water.

'They fuss over nothing,' said Robert, 'or maybe they're jealous.'

The feeling of claustrophobia he'd experienced as the hatch closed evaporated. Ed had been right, it felt as if they were in a bubble under the waves. It was cold perhaps, but the clear Cornish waters embraced the submersible and as his eyes adjusted to the change in light, Robert took in the soft golden sand and waving seaweed on submerged rocks. Crabs scuttled as the craft's shadow went over them. Small fish darted and Robert wondered if he'd have any success with a sea rod this time.

After a few minutes' instruction, he took control and steered the submersible further out under the waves.

'Does the sea-bed look much different?' said Bella.

Ed stopped taking readings to look outside, 'yes, actually yes it does.' He checked his watch and the oxygen levels, 'can you go over that way a little?'

Robert steered the submersible onwards. The water was darker now, the blue deeper, the swirling eddies green and they caught on rocks. He eased the power.

They travelled along the cliffs on either side. Caves faced each other across the cove, their floors were well underwater and would never be exposed even at the lowest tide. They visited the one on the left first. It seemed to be a deeper iridescent green than the dark waters. Even a long protruding rock was green, curving with sharp edges and regular fissures like pencil markings. Creatures zig-zagged under the sand across to the other cave. On their backs, spines appeared and disappeared. Tails flickered and then became invisible.

'What kind of fish are they?'

'No idea, never seen anything like it. Some sort of stone fish perhaps? Are you getting photos Bella?'

Bella operated the controls for the camera. Her glasses had misted up and she wasn't sure if she was focussing properly. In the current, the submersible rolled. The water swirled and sparkles of light flashed as if diamonds were suspended between the air above and sea below.

The cave on the other side looked different, almost blood red. Another long rock protruded but it was crimson.

'Iron oxide?'

'Don't think so, it's not the right geology. Trick of the light I expect.'

The zig-zagging creatures emerged from the sand and ran onto it, part camouflaged and moving too fast to see properly.

'Maybe they're amphibian,' said Bella.

'It's amazing how the motion of the water fools your eyes isn't it?' said Robert, 'I could have sworn that rock moved.'

He steered the submersible back into the middle of the cove where small boulders were piled up in the sand. He slowed and the craft bobbed.

'Yes, careful now,' said Ed, 'I know they're smooth, but any sort of rock is pretty treacherous, although I'm not sure what they're doing there. They look like the kind of stones you get from the back of a cave.'

'Hang on,' said Bella.

'Do you want to take over?' said Robert.

'No, it's not that. It's … look down there, something's sparkling.'

'Oh yes, I see what you mean!' said Robert, 'Ed, could you take over the controls and hold her steady? I'm just going to use the external arms to pick it up off the sea bed.'

He pressed levers and tensed, as the arms swung out from under the submersible and their pincers opened. Robert and Bella leaned forward as the mechanical hand reached down and lifted something with the delicacy of a duchess lifting a tea-cup. Grains of sand shifted and there was a vibration in the water.

'Gotcha!' said Robert, 'ready about! Land ahoy!'

*****

Rubrum murmurs: 'I heard that'
Viridi whispers: 'what? You heard nothing.'
Rubrum growls: 'I felt it then.'

*****

'Wait!' said Bella.

Ed held position, peering out into the waters.

'What is it?' said Robert.

'Look! Look where the sand's shifted, those creatures are back and the sea bed is moving.'

They peered around them, the submersible started to rock as the turbulence increased.

'This is weird,' said Ed, 'we'd better get back to land.'

'Earthquake? Surely not,' said Robert. He was focussed on the pincers, with its sparking find. But Bella was watching the shifting sand.

'Watch out!'

Something huge was sliding towards them: it zigzagged, lithe, green but massive. It came at such a speed it was blurred as it neared the pile of rocks below the submersible.

'Some kind of tremor must be pushing up rocks from under the surface!' said Ed, engaging the throttle and starting to turn, 'we've got to get back to land!'

Bella rubbed her glasses, 'it's not a rock,' she argued, 'it's alive. It's got legs and…'

The creature reached the rocks. A tail, perhaps two metres in length encircled them and obscured the glimmer in the sand. Its face, shaped like an arrow head raised from the sea bed and stared into the submersible. Eyes of amber blinked. They were flecked with emerald and trimmed with long thick eyelashes like curled copper wire. Spines of narrow jade flint lifted along the creature's back.

'It's a dragon!' said Ed, 'but…they don't exist!'

The creature frowned and opened her mouth. Green sparks nearly blinded them and a huge clawed foot lifted from the sand and struck the side of the submersible.

They spun in the water over and over. Ed's head hit the side with a clunk and he slumped, eyes closed. Robert pushed him sideways and grabbed the controls.

This is not a time to feel sea-sick, he told himself firmly. Bella was trying to focus the camera on the dragon but the rolling made it impossible. Robert gripped the rudder as if it was the last cream cake in the patisserie and prayed for strength. The rolling was lessening, the power was kicking in. As they righted and he turned towards land, Bella looked back.

'There's another, stop!'

Below them something even bigger was zig-zagging towards the pile of rocks. It was a deep crimson with spines of garnet. It reached the green dragon and tried to uncoil her tail with his own. But she pointed with a claw and he turned, fixing the submersible with a rugby ball sized ruby eye flecked with rose quartz.

'Can you get a photo?' said Robert, 'what do you reckon, F5, 1/160th, ISO 320?'

'Forget the photograph!' yelled Bella, 'we're about to get eaten by a dragon - get us out of here!'

He opened up the throttle as red sparks followed them through the water.

*****

Viridi sulks: 'it said I didn't exist'

Rubrum comforts: 'never mind my sweet, my luscious, how the sea brings out the colour of your eyes'
Viridi remembers: 'yesterday, you called me old'
Rubrum qualifies: 'but my darling, in context, we are old compared to them but thankfully we are not human. And, my lovely, my gorgeous, we are still young and full of fire, mere youths and you don't look a day over one thousand.'
Viridi mumbles: 'you're just saying that, you and your smooth Welsh tongue. Before the storm, you said my bum looked big.'
Rubrum cajoles: 'I never did, you misheard me, I said your curves filled your cave. It's not the same at all. A dragon should fill a cave. It's what caves are for. Is that why you hid my hoard? Because you misunderstood my meaning? My pretty, my lovely, you are more precious than a fleet of sinking pirate-ships to me.'
Viridi pouts: 'Am I? Am I still? You wouldn't prefer a younger lizard with smoother scales?'
Rubrum chuckles: 'No, I want a real dragoness. Come and give me a kiss'
Viridi tips her head on the side and considers. She moves from the rocks and pushes them aside to reveal a pile of gold and silver, miniatures and strings of pearls and gemstones.
Rubrum frowns, he tries to count, but his mate is humming and when he turns, her eyelashes flutter and she blows heart-shaped smoke rings through the water. He looks around for the small creatures.
Rubrum commands: 'back to the cave kids. Mother and father… have things to discuss…oh and Las, go to the village and tell them all is well.'
The little dragons zig zag back across the sand out of sight.
Viridi and Rubrum touch snouts and their eyes close in delight as they entwine on the horde.
Rubrum whispers: 'see? The spark is still there.'
And for a while, the sea around flickers with gold and flashes of ruby and emerald.
*****

Kyle was waiting with ropes by the steps when the submersible resurfaced. Jane and Laura were sitting on the wall beside him, leaning forward. It had been hard to track the craft's progress around the cove but in the last few minutes when it got to the middle, the water had churned and bubbled and now it seemed as if the midday sun refracting through the sea was creating an optical illusion. It was as if a firework display was taking place under water.

The hatch opened and Bella was helped out by Kyle. She wobbled a little as she hugged her daughters. Jane and Kyle reached in to support Robert onto dry land and Laura handed him his walking sticks. Balancing on one, he waved the other towards the sea, his mouth opening and shutting but nothing coming out.

'Are you all right Dad?' said Laura, putting her arms round his shoulders.

Ed emerged next, rubbing his head and pausing to stare back out over the cove.

'Mate,' he murmured to Kyle, 'we gotta talk.'

'Is there something wrong with the submersible?'

'No, it did a fabulous job, as did Robert. It's something else altogether.'

'Good or bad?'

'No idea, get your Cornish gran on the phone. We need some intel.'

'Gran? What do old people know… I mean… hang on what's that in the pincer?'

Kyle winched the submersible out of the water and reached for the grabbing mechanism. It was gripping a gold coin.

'What the…?'

Robert peered at it, '"Hisp… 1588"? Armada. Bet you anything. That'll pay for some more equipment. Could you get us some coffee Laura? Then we can see what we managed to get on film. Come on Bella,' they made their way to the changing area. It would be good to get into some sensible trousers and a proper straw hat. They both swayed as they walked.

Jane sat down at the table, waiting for everyone to join her. The men were checking over the submersible and whispering to each other, turning the coin over in their hands. Ed was waving his arms and Kyle was scratching his head. Laura had gone inside to get coffees from the bar. Sooner or later someone would tell her what was going on, but in the meantime, she'd just soak up the sun.

A lizard run up the slipway and across the courtyard. She'd never seen anything like it. It was around the size of an iguana and an iridescent blue, as if lapis lazuli had become flesh. It paused, shook sea-water from its body and small sapphire spines lifted along its back.

Catching sight of Jane, it zig-zagged towards her and staring up said, 'parents huh?'

A puff of indigo smoke came out of its mouth and then it opened slender turquoise wings and flew off towards the village.

Jane still had her mouth open when Laura came out.

'Cat got your tongue?'

'Not cat, dragon.'

'Sorry what?'

'Dragon. I just saw a dragon. It was about this size and blue.'

'Of course you did.'

Robert and Bella joined them and sat down.

'How was the dive Dad?' said Laura, giving up on her sister.

'Fantastic,' said Dad, 'in fact, I'd go as far as to say it was legendary.'

Ed and Kyle came over to sit down.

'My gran says the dragons do this every twenty years or so. They have a row, make up, settle down. She says the better the fireworks under water, the longer they'll be mellow.'

Everyone looked at the cove. The surface of the water was exploding with colour.

'Never thought I'd meet dragons at my time of life,' said Bella.

‘Dragons? What dragons?’ said Laura, ‘it’s not fair! You’ve all seen dragons except me!’

‘Best get underwater then,’ said Robert.

‘Where are those wetsuits?’ said Laura, pushing back her coffee, ‘get me in that submersible! Show me the controls!’

‘I’ll show you,’ said Ed.

‘Me too, me too!’ said Jane.

‘Typical,’ said Laura.

Dad - The Trencherman

Orange and Beige

1973 Autumn - I remember

We went to the Wimpy Bar before going to the fair. We perused the glossy menu just like we did every time, even though we always ate the same things and they never turned up looking quite like they did in the photographs. Apart from Mum, who insisted on gammon and pineapple, the rest of us ate burgers. There was something decadent about eating them, even with a knife and fork. The chips were thinner than normal and a large tomato had been cut in half and frightened by a grill. It was exotic and American.

Dad said that eating before we went to the fair would stop us from wanting anything sweet.

The fair started with a sort of market trailing along the High Street, blocking the pane glass of Woolworths and the tobacconists. A Cockney stood on a stool selling china, shuffling plates without breaking them, flinging them into the air and then catching them, his eyes on the crowd, his patter constant and mesmerising.

'Better than Marks and Sparks, better than Selfridges, fine china fit for the Queen, come on darlin', git yore ol man to spoil yer. Look at the quality, look at the sheen, you could read a paper fru this plate. Going for an 'undred in 'arrods but I ain't selling for an 'undred, I ain't selling for fifty, I ain't selling for twenty…'

I loved hearing the flat East-end tones and dry humour but crockery, however skilfully manhandled, was not what I was interested in.

Round the end of the town, near Boots and WH Smith's and the little shop which sold Welsh crafts, the fair had bloomed into a smoky gaudy mass of metal, music and shouting. The wild boys from down the hill said their absent Dad was from the fair people. They blamed him for their roaming, their dislike of the classroom. I tried to see someone who looked similar in the strangers taking money on the rides, but it was hard to get a true idea of their faces.

At the rifle range, Dad paid for us each to take a shot at the row of trundling ducks.

'I can't understand it, I'm the one who's a good shot,' he complained when his third attempt failed but Jane managed to flatten three in a row and win a wonky eyed Mickey Mouse.

He cheered himself up by buying us all candy floss.

'How much would it be to get a candy floss machine Dad?' I asked.

It seemed so economical, just one teaspoon of coloured sugar and some spinning resulted in a cloud of infinite sweetness on a stick. It didn't even taste like sugar, but almost like toffee or honey or... it had always melted on my tongue before I could work it out.

Candy floss stuck round Dad's mouth like lipstick and then disappeared. Jane had some in her hair and she was pinching bits of it to squash them into wedges of pink candy. Her fingers and cheeks were stained and sticky.

'Toffee apple?' tempted a woman at a stall. In the early dusk, the apples glistened. So red, so glossy. Dismissing all thoughts of Snow White's stepmother, I paid over my pennies. Surely this year... Biting through the toffee as hard as glass and then ... just the same as before: another soft and withered apple underneath.

Dad took us on the bumper cars, Mum and Jane in one and him and me in another. A slow start and then we were off.

'Women drivers!' he yelled as we crashed head-on.

I took the wheel, sitting on the very edge of the seat to reach the pedal. Overhead the electricity flashed and pop music blared around us. A lanky teenage boy danced between the cars, never quite looking at anyone, cool to the yells and screams and laughter, taking control when people stalled to get them going again, jumping from car to car as if they were bulls and he was dancing between them. Then the power died. Dizzy and jolted, we clambered off, laughing.

'Who's for the waltzers?'

I shook my head, so he took Jane and they spiralled away from us on the rolling, rotating track while another indifferent fairground boy rode the undulations and spun the seats. They appeared and disappeared in a whirl of colour. Jane's face was only just above the bar but Dad was like a king next to her grinning and laughing.

Then they got off and Jane, after staggering for a bit, threw up behind the hook-a-duck stall.

It was getting dark. The lights on the rides were no longer subtle against smoky grey skies but gaudy against the night. Teenage girls in gaggles, comparing flared jeans and denim jackets, whispered and sidled near to the rides.

The fairground boys kept taking money and kick-starting dodgems but their insolent indifference had been replaced by appraising sideways glances, a straightening of muscled shoulders and rolling up of sleeves to expose tanned arms. The girls giggled, playing with their hair and blowing bubble gum through pale lipsticked lips, their eyes flicking, half-listening to each other, alert for the second glance, the offer of a light. The red glow of cigarettes flared and softened. Local teenage boys called to them, mocking with their childhood schoolyard nicknames but the girls for the most part ignored them, and the boys swaggered onto the bumper cars where they drove at each other with the fury of a joust. But their pale skin and familiar faces could not distract the girls' attention from the lure of the enigmatic incomers.

The thunder of the generators and cacophony of music, the shouts of the teenagers and the screams from the big wheel and the waltzers; the jeers and jibes of the spurned local lads and the unreadable stares of the fairground boys all throbbed with the flashing lights and something else, a current under it all that I didn't quite understand. It was something dangerous and exciting like wanting to put your finger into a candle flame but being afraid of the pain.

The families were all going away, leaving the fair to the hidden, secret world of youth. It was time to go home.

*****

On Saturday morning we went down to breakfast.

The table looked a little bare. There was usually a filled toast rack, the butter dish and marmalade jar and Dad was usually in the kitchen grilling bacon and frying eggs in fat so hot the white went frilly and crispy.

Today Dad was in the kitchen but there was no sound of sizzling, just the serious burble of Radio 4. Mum poured coffee for Jane and tea for me and sat back with her own, sipping and frowning. I looked round. There was something missing. I got up and looked inside the sideboard.

'Where's the sugar, Mum?'

'Dad says we're to stop putting it in our drinks.'

'Why?' asked Jane, wincing at the bitterness of her coffee.

'Because,' said Dad, coming in to place half a grapefruit on each of our places, 'we're on a diet.'

We all stared at him. At this time, I should point out, Jane, Mum and I were small and thin. In December, with a fake white beard, Dad was in demand as Father Christmas.

'You've forgotten to lay the spoons,' said Dad delving in the sideboard drawer.

The only exciting thing about grapefruit was the spoons. They were silver, a peculiar shape like a leaf with a pointed end. They were perfect for scooping out segments which would have been so much nicer sprinkled with brown sugar and grilled.

I sipped my tea and wondered how long it would take to get used to it unsweetened.

'And there's a new restaurant opened up in town, I thought we'd try it for lunch when we're doing our shopping. It's very modern,' he said to me and Jane, 'very … er … trendy.'

We cringed, as you do when your father tries to sound … er … trendy.

'And,' he added, eyeing up the grapefruit Jane was struggling to eat, 'I managed to catch the milkman this morning and I've put in an order for yoghurt every day. And just in case that's not enough, I'm going to make a yoghurt machine this afternoon. I read about it in a magazine. All I need is a heated pad and a jug.'

'But we all hate yoghurt Dad,' I pointed out.

'Nonsense, it's very healthy, we just need to change our eating habits.'

'But…'

'No arguing,' he said, pouring himself more coffee and downing it with only a slight wince, 'I got on the scales this morning and realised something needed to be done.'

'Robert, I've been telling you that for years,' said Mum.

It was true. Up until now though, Jane and I had defended Dad's figure on the grounds that it was cuddly. Up until now though, no-one had suggested losing weight might be a family exercise.

After breakfast, we went into town and parked a little further from the shops than normal and walked up the hill towards the main commercial district. The buildings on the lower part of the incline were, shop-fronts aside, much as they had been for a couple of hundred years having somehow been missed when the city was bombed in 1941. They were tall and narrow with pointed roofs, a little like Dutch houses and might have been attractive if the area hadn't looked so unloved.

We stopped at the Italian delicatessen. It was dark inside and smelled pungent with the scented ghosts of spice and herbs. Near the counter were sacks of dried pulses. Chickpeas tumbled in yellow profusion, lentils slithered. Dad selected a long blue packet of spaghetti and asked for some tomato purée and a small container with dried Parmesan.

'May we also have a pound of chickpeas, a pound of lentils, two pounds of basmati and some chapatti flour too please?' he went on.

Jane and I exchanged glances.

Outside, heading on up the hill, Mum remonstrated, 'I wish you wouldn't get that tomato purée, I hate mince and onions messed up.'

'And that Parmesan smells of sick,' pointed out Julia, 'and tastes like poo.'

'Jane,' warned Dad.

She ignored him and went on, 'can't we have tinned meatballs and cheddar cheese on the spaghetti like other people?'

'Don't be silly,' said Dad, 'the point is that the tomatoes and Parmesan are authentic.'

'Isn't spaghetti fattening?' said Mum.

'Nonsense, it's just flour and water.'

Mum prodded the packages of pulses, 'and these are a nuisance too, they take ages to rinse clean and I don't know what to do with them.'

'Indian food. I've been reading up on Indian food. We can have a lentil curry with rice and chapattis. Don't worry, I'll cook it all.'

'Do you know how?'

'Can't be that hard, boil it all up and put in some curry powder I expect. And chapattis are fun. You can cook them over the gas flame I think.'

None of this sounded appealing or safe. Dad had already scorched the tiles on the kitchen ceiling when trying to flambé pancakes in brandy.

'I'm working up quite an appetite,' said Dad, 'but let's be disciplined. Bookshop first.'

I would have preferred to go to WH Smith's with its modern children's books. But Dad preferred the old shop down Lustrous Passage, where behind dusty windows, books in brown and green tooled covers with gilt edges huddled in heaps looking down on dog-eared orange and white penguin paperbacks. To be fair, no modern shop could compete with that smell of old paper and ancient ink. Opening a volume to see if there were any pictures, looking for the ſ's in place of s's in the middle of words. It was impossible to read them without pronouncing them as f's. I imagined a sentence of my own: 'My ſister is a ſtupenouſly ſtupid ſlimy ſlug who ſquaſhes ſtrawberries with her ſummer ſandals'.

After half an hour during which he bought only two books, we continued up the hill towards the ruined castle and modern shopping area. 1950s and 60s grey angular concrete buildings stood in uniform utility across the street from a Tudor building with curlicued gables.

The Tudor building was a shop with uneven floors and fancy goods. It was beautiful but our hearts belonged to Woolworths, which occupied a carbuncle in front of the castle and the cinema. Hopefully, Jane and I stepped towards it. There was the vague chance of buying some clackers to replace the ones Dad had shattered when trying to prove that school was wrong to ban them because of the risk of shattering.

But Dad steered us towards the indoor market.

'Lunch time!' he said, 'and it'll be a new experience!'

I don't know if the 1970s were really orange and beige or whether something went wrong when all the photographs were developed, but that is my recollection and the most orange and beige experience of my life was that lunch.

The restaurant was on an upper floor with a cheerful sign in groovy script decorated in stylised flowers. 'Health Food!' it promised, 'Vegetarian! Wholefoods!'

Inside the restaurant was an abundance of pine. There were pine benches and tables, pine clad walls, a pine clad ceiling. A woman with wild curly hair barely controlled by a scarf stood behind the counter. A young man wearing wide flares was clearing dirty crockery. Dad eyed the young man's long hair in disapproval but cheered when he saw that the food was self service, laid out in dishes along the counter so that you could choose what you wanted and pile your plate high.

The trouble was that I would only have wanted any of it if I'd had long ears and a fluffy tail.

In the orange section there was grated carrot, boiled lentils of varying types, raw swede. In the beige section there were raw mushrooms, various grains, boiled chickpeas and brown rice. In the almost interesting section there were spring onions, bean sprouts and cress. This must have been the one and only time in my life when I'd have preferred a school dinner.

'Come on!' said Dad, 'fill your plates! You must be hungry. I am.'

We sat down at a long table and looked at our lunch, waiting for it to look appetising.

'What's that?' Jane said, pointing at a psychedelic poster behind Dad. When he and Mum turned, she pushed her raw mushrooms onto his plate. I wished I'd thought of it.

Up until that point, raw food in my experience had been a summer time thing, namely salad. It was unnatural to be eating it in September. We sat and chewed our way through powdery pulses and claggy rice. Grated carrots, which I normally loathed, were at least sweet. The beansprouts tasted of soap and earnestness. Dad shovelled it all down regardless. We had yet to find the thing he wouldn't eat. Eventually he went to pay and came back with yet more packages.

'We can grow our own beansprouts!' he informed us, 'and mushrooms. All we need is a warm dark corner.'

'I'm not sure I want to eat beansprouts and mushrooms every day,' said Mum.

'Nonsense, they're healthy. Only,' Dad dropped his voice to a whisper, 'we'll cook the mushrooms, I'm not sure about them raw.'

At home, he made his yoghurt maker and laid it out along the sideboard in the absence of any space elsewhere. He made a lentil curry with the turmeric which Mum used to colour kedgeree. The chapattis were, he was right, fun. Once he got the mixture right.

'No point in measuring!' he declared, but nearly blocked the gas jets with the resulting gloop. Mum made him cook them in the frying pan. The curry tasted of grit and despair.

'Maybe I didn't put enough powder in,' he wondered.

For dinner the next day we had our usual roast chicken but had to have boiled potatoes instead of roast. We had the homemade yoghurt for pudding, at which point Dad had got the sugar bowl out of hiding and said that we'd stick to the stuff the milkman brought in future.

On Monday, I came home from school alone.

'Where's Jane?' said Mum.

'She's gone to Julie's for tea.'

'What do you mean "she's gone to Julie's for tea"?' said Mum, 'and who's Julie?'

I closed my eyes and tried to remember which of my sister's gang was Julie. They all looked much the same. Sometimes I chased them about being a monster at Jane's request, but mostly I kept to the juniors' playground and they kept to the infants'.

'I think she's the one with dark hair.'

'Well, what's her surname? Where does she live?'

I shrugged, 'I think she lives near the school.'

The school was a bus ride away.

'Are they on the phone?'

It was pointless asking me. I didn't even know how many people in my own class were on the phone, let alone any numbers. It was unthinkable that we'd ever ring each other up. The phone was for adults and sufficiently expensive that Dad had invested in a cassette recorder so that we could record long monologues for our grandparents as it was cheaper to post them than have the phone-call.

'Go and ask Ffion's Mum if she knows,' Mum ordered.

Half an hour later Jane, unrepentant, was delivered home by Julie's father. Not only unrepentant but furious.

'What were you thinking of?' demanded Mum, 'you know you don't go round to people's houses unless the parents have agreed it.'

'Julie *asked* me,' argued Jane.

'I thought you didn't like Julie very much,' I said.

'I don't, but they were having macaroni cheese with crispy bacon on top with apple pie and custard for pudding.'

She had a point. Dad had rung Mum earlier from work to say he would be cooking dinner. We laid the table in gloom and some trepidation.

At six-thirty we sat down and were served a beige poached egg swimming in brown liquid with beansprouts as a garnish and a doorstep of buttered bread.

Jane and I looked at each other and then at Dad.

'Come on, eat up!' he said, 'it's a Middle-Eastern recipe: eggs poached in vinegar. It'll be lovely.'

It wasn't. It was even worse than school dinners.

Gagging on the first mouthful, my eyes watered. Surely, surely this time Dad wouldn't insist I finish my plateful.

'Robert?'

I looked up at Dad. He was eyeing his own food with confusion and his knife and fork were suspended.

'It tastes like sick,' said Jane.

Dad didn't contradict her this time. He put his knife and fork down, got up and cleared the table.

'Go and watch TV for a bit,' he said, 'I'm going out. We'll eat later.'

Jane and I washed up the dishes as we watched Dad drive off back down the hill.

'I never, ever thought there was anything in the whole world Dad wouldn't eat,' I said.

'Me neither,' said Jane, 'I'm so hungry. If Mum hadn't made me come home from Julie's, we might be on second helpings of pudding by now. And why have I always got to do the drying up?'

Half an hour later Dad reappeared with a Chinese takeaway

The special fried rice was salty, the little shrimps pink and chewy, the peas sweet, the egg in tiny strips of pale yellow. Spring rolls and sweet and sour pork dripped with oil. Prawn crackers melted on our mouths like salty fizzing rice paper. Spare-ribs glistened. Chicken in soy sauce was brightened with spring onion and *cooked* beansprouts. Dad brought out the chopsticks and piled his plate high.

'I've decided that diet I put us on was perhaps a little bland,' said Dad, 'and besides, I haven't lost any weight.'

'I'm not surprised,' said Mum, 'you only started on Saturday, you kept eating up the children's leftovers and you wolfed three hazelnut yogurts this morning on the grounds no-one else likes them.'

Dad ignored her, 'so it's back to normal and on payday we'll go to the Berni Inn and I'll have roast duck and green peas.'

'So that's the end of healthy eating then Dad,' I said, licking spare-rib sauce from my lips.

'Well, we'll stick to coffee and tea without sugar,' he said after a moment, 'that'll get rid of a few pounds. And besides, everyone knows roast duck and green peas are healthy. Peas are full of vitamins and duck is full of...er... iron. Anyway, are you going to finish that chicken or shall I?'

'Please tell me this is the end of the fads, Robert,' said Mum.

'I don't have fads,' said Dad, eyeing up my plate, 'I have plans and the latest one is to do with clothes.'

We stared at him. Dad's fashion sense, such as it was, had stopped in 1956.

'I haven't had a chance to tell you yet but John's bringing something round for you later Bella. I know you'll like it, what with all the sewing you do.'

Mum lowered her fork and narrowed her eyes. She waited.

'It's a loom. John's wife didn't want it, so I said you'd have it. Might be a bit of a squeeze in the kitchen but it'll be fine. You can weave your own cloth. It'll be wonderful.'

'Good,' said Mum to our surprise. Then she added, 'I could do with some garters and now I can use your guts to make some.'

Hospital Food

2012 Wednesday

Dad is quieter. He is not moving a great deal though his eyes flicker when we talk.

> *We hold his hand and pray.*
> *Jane says, 'find a psalm, Laura.'*
> *I read Psalm 23:*

'The Lord is my shepherd, I lack nothing.
'He makes me lie down in green pastures,
'he leads me beside quiet waters, he refreshes my soul.
'He guides me along the right paths for his name's sake.
'Even though I walk through the darkest valley,
'I will fear no evil, for you are with me;
'your rod and your staff, they comfort me.
'You prepare a table before me in the presence of my enemies.
'You anoint my head with oil; my cup overflows.
'Surely your goodness and love will follow me all the days of my life,
'and I will dwell in the house of the Lord forever.'

> *Dad's eyes flicker more wildly.*
> *'Perhaps you're reading the wrong version' says Jane.*
> *'What do you want me to cook when you come round?' I say, squeezing Dad's hand.*

> *I have long since learned to love healthy eating. Perhaps it wasn't the health food's restauranteurs' fault. There wasn't as much to choose from in those days and not many people knew what to do with exotic ingredients if they were available. Or maybe it's just that tastes change over time.*

> *I am now a good cook and love cooking. And thanks to growing up in clutter, I can cook a three course meal in a space only big enough for a chopping board. This has come in handy on many a camping trip.*

> *Jane, fortunately for her family, married someone who is a good cook and loves cooking. She could burn water.*

Like Dad, I enjoy trying new recipes and cuisines; love to tell him what I've been cooking, describe the flavours, argue over ingredients. It broke my heart when he said he no longer enjoyed eating. Dad without an appetite is like summer without sunshine.

Now, in emotional limbo, cooking is the only thing I can control. There is no time to declutter the bungalow, there are no words to comfort Mum, there is nothing I can do to make Dad come round. I can plan and organise and boss to my heart's content and it will make no difference.

I don't want to eat and nor do Jane and Mum, but we need to. Caring for them all is the only practical thing I can do.

'I'll look after Mum,' I'd promised Dad on Saturday, 'don't worry, everything will be fine.'

This week, everything tastes as bland and cardboard-like as that whole-food from long ago. On Friday, whether Dad has come round or is still unconscious, I'll cook something garlicky and salty and full of taste and maybe the flavour will cut through our worry.

'Dad, do you remember when you made chilli con carne for the first time?' says Jane, 'you got your teaspoons and tablespoons mixed up for the chilli powder. Our mouths were on fire for hours.'

'Nowadays, a tablespoon would be nothing,' I say, 'a chilli can't be too hot.'

'Speak for yourself,' says Mum, 'I still prefer plain mince and onions with some mashed potato.'

'Dad, do you remember when you caught on to the wine-making phase,' says Jane, 'only a kit from Boots wasn't good enough and you started making them up out of a book?'

'Oh, that rice wine was disgusting,' I pull a face in recollection, 'you said it would taste like saké, not that any of us would have known whether it did or not.'

'The last one I remember was the cherry wine he made when I was fifteen. That was good,' Jane recalls, 'we drank it while we were playing a game of cards I think.'

'Oh I remember!' I say, 'and we were all so tipsy, we were laughing too much to care who won.'

'I beat you,' says Jane.

'Bet you didn't'

'Bet I did.'

'Dad, do you remember when Jane made you that Guinness cake and got the measurements all wrong?' I say.

'I remember that!' says Mum, 'we cooked it for three whole hours in the oven, and it was **still** liquid!'

'You tried to drink it Dad, didn't you?' I go on, 'but even **you** couldn't manage beer flavoured cake batter.'

'Hey!' says Jane, '**anyone** could get one pint and four fluid ounces muddled up.'

Dad twitches but sleeps on, still dreaming...

Dad tells himself a story….

Stars

TEXTS
JANE: Dad asked me for a recipe
LAURA: You can't cook
JANE: I know. I was running late. I made something up
LAURA: Oh great, you'll poison them
JANE: Cheek
LAURA: He asked me for a recipe too. What's he's up to?
JANE: Don't know. When should we start worrying?

LAURA: When did you STOP worrying?

*****

Bronwen the TV producer took a deep breath and pulled the tablet out of her bag. She knew her idea for a TV programme would be the making of her. A brilliant idea, unique and…

'It's all been done before,' mumbled Giles. He was still trembling from the almost perpendicular ascent to the estate. There had been a few hairy moments when the sat nav had instructed them to go the wrong direction up a one way street at forty-five degrees to sea-level with the engine crying for mercy. Fortunately no-one had been coming the other way.

'No it hasn't,' Bronwen argued, 'anyway, all you've got to do is work out where the cameras will go.'

She got out of the car and eyed number 30, then turned round to look at the view, which as the bungalow clung to the side of the hill, was impressive. Giles gauged the width of the road and shuddered.

'How will we get the equipment up here?'

'Stop being negative,' said Bronwen, 'I'm sure you'll work out all the details.'

An elderly man peering out of the window, waggled his fingers at her and an elderly woman appeared at the door.

'Bronwen and Giles,' Bronwen said as they shook hands and stepped into the bungalow, 'so pleased to meet you.'

Giles was measuring up the hall with a laser and jotting things down on his laptop, which he balanced on a few fingers.

'That'll have to go,' he said, indicating a bookcase, stuffed to within an inch of its life and topped by a selection of photographs, ornaments and souvenirs. He peered at a very old, moth-eaten moggy curled up amongst them, 'er… I think your cat may be dead.'

'Don't worry dear,' said the elderly woman, 'it usually sits on the dashboard but the car's been in for a service.'

She offered no further information and led them towards the main room.

118

'That'll have to go too,' Giles pointed at a carved footstool with a large plant on it, behind which a photograph of four children was propped at an angle as if they were trying to hide in the jungle.

'Never mind that just now,' said Bronwen. She followed the other woman into the living room and gasped.

'I know,' said the elderly man, 'the vista is stunning isn't it? You can just make out the sea.'

But Bronwen's gaze wasn't aimed through the window. She stared round the room with her mouth open. There was a dining table, a three piece suite, six book cases, a TV and any amount of boxes. On a low coffee table was some embroidery in a hoop and propped against a sideboard was a tapestry. Large photographs in mounts were squeezed between the sofa and one of the armchairs. There was, perhaps, five square feet of unoccupied floor.

The man got up and pushed some paperwork aside so she could sit down on the sofa. She closed her mouth and smiled.

'Well, er thank you Mr and Mrs Darrow,' she started.

'Do call us Robert and Bella.'

'Of course, well, thank you for asking to take part in "Masterhost". As you know it's a brand new programme and we're keen to get filming started. It is going to be a completely new take on cookery programmes. As participants, you will host a dinner, provide your guests with a three course meal and at the end the public will phone in to vote. Your application was extremely interesting. Fusion cuisine is very trendy right now. But I wasn't quite clear which traditions you were fusing, I wonder if you could elaborate by telling me your menu.'

Robert got up and rummaged on the coffee table, then handed over a document in inked script.

Appetiser: Gwilym-tong

Starter: Caldo Verde com explosão

Entrée: Jamburnsalaya

Pudding: Guinless Cake

To drink: Home-made Sock-blaster

'Er...' said Bronwen.

'I've always been interested in cooking,' said Robert, indicating a bookcase bulging with recipe books, 'but I thought I'd get all the girls to contribute. Make it a family thing.'

'Has he got a harem?' whispered Giles, 'cos if he does, that might improve the programme.'

'He's over seventy years old,' Bronwen whispered back, 'but I suppose if *he's* got a harem, there's hope for you to get a girlfriend yet.'

Giles grunted.

'All what girls?' said Bronwen aloud, checking her notes, 'it says here you have two daughters.'

'That's right, Laura and Jane,' said Robert, 'then there are Ines and Clara.'

'Who are…?'

'We're sort of in loco parentis. They're from abroad.'

'So they're foster children.'

'No they're about forty.'

Bronwen waited for more explanation. None came.

'I expected Laura and Jane to come up with British dishes, but they didn't. So I decided to fuse everything together and give them a English/Scottish/Irish/Welsh feel in honour of our ancestry.'

'Mind you, it's was a bit of a risk asking Jane,' said Bella, 'you should have asked her husband. He's a chef.'

'That wouldn't be as much fun.'

'Jane says pasta is a vegetable on the basis that it's made from wheat,' Bella told Bronwen, 'and she argues that cheese originates from grass, sugar comes from a plant and chocolate is fundamentally a bean. She says that macaroni cheese followed by chocolate ice-cream therefore constitutes four of her five a day.'

'Jane always was a girl after my own heart,' said Robert with pride, 'and she's sent her old recipe for Guinness cake. I'm adapting it. It may be more of a mousse than a pudding.'

Giles nudged Bronwen until she shut her mouth again.

'We were a bit worried about Laura's contribution,' Robert continued, 'her cooking is generally beyond the Scoville scale. Her husband even puts chillies on roast potatoes. And if it's not spice, then it's pulses. That fabada she'd cooked once Bella, do you remember? How many days was it till we stopped …'

'Whatever's wrong with good plain British cooking?' said Bella, 'boiled ham, boiled potatoes and cabbage; mince and mashed potatoes, poached fish and…'

'Bit boring,' said Robert.

'So,' interrupted Bronwen in an effort to regain control, 'the names of the dishes are rather, er, unusual. For example, what's Gwilym-tong?'

'It's in honour of South Africa, where Clara comes from.'

'Robert wanted to make scrambled ostrich egg,' said Bella, 'but we weren't sure where to get one and anyway, I haven't got a pan big enough. Besides, I refuse to spend three days trying to get the burnt bits off afterwards.'

Giles had wandered off to work out whether it would be possible to film in the kitchen. It wouldn't be. It was hard to imagine how two people could get in there at the same time, let alone a camera crew. There was a jar of something on the window-sill. Small lumps were just discernible in a murky liquid. Every now and then one of them appeared to jerk and then collapse. He brought the jar into the sitting-room.

'I think your tadpoles are dying,' he said.

'You're a little obsessed with death,' said Bella, 'do you think you should talk to someone?'

'It's actually very much alive,' said Robert, waggling his eyebrows, 'and it's all my own!'

Giles stopped unscrewing the lid and paled, 'please tell me it's not a sample of body fluids!'

The contents of the jar lurched.

'No, of course not. It's a plant. But it could do with feeding. We'll wait till you're gone.'

'Are your guests supposed to eat it?'

Robert raised his eyebrows 'no of course not. They'll be drinking it.'

'Of course they will,' muttered Giles, taking the jar back into the kitchen at arm's length.

'Er…' said Bronwen, 'going back to Gwilym-tong…'

'You've heard of biltong haven't you? It's South African dried meat. Well this will be biltong made with strips of Welsh beef.'

'Er…'

'Gwilym. It's Welsh for William. Will… Bill… bill-tong… biltong. Never mind. Anyway, it's pretty windy round here so I *was* thinking of drying the strips of beef outside the back door but…'

'This is South Wales and it rains half the time,' said Giles.

'Well yes,' confessed Robert, 'so I'm going to dry it in the airing cupboard instead.'

'No you're not,' said Bella.

'Don't worry, it'll be fine,' said Robert.

*****

TEXTS

LAURA: Did you get a call from someone called Bronwen?
JANE: Yup
LAURA: Dad's going to be on TV. Cooking.
JANE: Yup.
LAURA: Have you started worrying yet?
JANE: Oh yes.

*****

The day of filming had arrived. Bronwen had rejected the idea of recording the programme. It would have so much more energy if it went out live.

Now, watching Giles set up, periodically admonished for swearing by Robert, she had a faint yearning for the cutting room. *No, be strong,* she told herself, *this show will make your career.*

Emptying the sitting room of all but the dining table and chairs had taken three days of negotiations and one day of transference to a large storage unit. It didn't seem possible that

122

the room could have held so much stuff without exploding. What with that and the mysterious jam jar, which seemed to have disappeared, Giles muttered that he thought the Darrows were possibly aliens living on some sort of space-time anomaly and that they were filming the wrong genre. Robert was still complaining that the room no longer had any character.

'You're as bad as Laura,' he said, 'she always says it's too messy. I can't understand it, she never seemed to mind when she was growing up.'

'She can't talk anyway. Her house isn't exactly minimalist,' added Bella, 'people who live in glass houses…'

'… "should lower the blinds when removing their trousers"…' said Robert happily.

'Er…' said Bronwen.

'Spike Milligan,' said Robert, 'you young people don't seem to know anything. It's such a shame I haven't got the Goon Show on CD. We could have played them for atmosphere, couldn't we Bella?'

'No,' said Bella.

Robert started singing 'I'm walking backwards for Christmas, across the Irish Sea!'

Bronwen felt her teeth grate.

'Maybe classical?' she suggested, 'what do you think?'

'Bit boring,' said Robert, 'I'll find something.'

'Right, so…' said Bronwen, 'your guests will be arriving shortly and then we'll start filming.'

'Who are the guests again?' asked Bella, 'didn't you say it was the mayor, the food writer from the South Wales Echo and that TV chef who lives in the Gower?'

Bronwen shrugged, 'this is a new programme, so we couldn't get all the people we'd have liked. So we've got the cookery teacher from the high school, the food critic for The Gazette…'

'I didn't know The Gazette had a food page,' interrupted Robert, 'or I'd have read it.'

'It's more of a sort of paragraph,' said Bronwen, 'so we've got the teacher, the critic and instead of the TV chef, we've got a food blogger from Neath.'

'Oh, well that should be all right,' said Bella. She readjusted the flowers and straightened the glasses, 'I'll bet they've never had anything like this meal.'

'I'll bet *no-one* has,' said Giles under his breath as he passed to check some lighting.

'I'm surprised your daughters and er…"girls" didn't want to be here. People usually can't wait to be on TV.'

'They said they wanted to watch it live and get the full viewer experience,' said Robert, standing up from the CD player, 'I was afraid they might forget to tell all their friends to watch, so I texted them all and tagged them all on Facebook. Laura didn't seem too happy. I did think of asking if the grandchildren could be waiters and then I thought about it a bit harder.'

He didn't elaborate. He wandered off into the kitchen as the guests arrived and 'My Old Man's a Dustman!' started booming from the speakers.

'Roll 'em!' said Giles.

Robert placed a plate of something thin, flat and brown in front of each guest. It had been a struggle as he was using his stick to walk and simultaneously carrying three plates. There had been some slippage and a sprig of parsley garnish had fallen to the floor.

'Voilà!' he declared, 'Gwilym-tong!'

The guests simultaneously leaned forward and peered.

'It looks like a beef burger that's been sat on,' said the teacher. The blogger took a photo on her phone and took some notes.

'Marinated cow-pat?' suggested the food critic.

Robert frowned, 'certainly not. It's biltong made following a traditional South African recipe but using Welsh beef.'

'What recipe did you follow?' asked the blogger, her pen poised. The critic went to spear his portion and found that the fork couldn't pierce the meat. It shot across the table and into the lap of the cookery teacher.

'Well, when I say "followed", we followed it up until the ingredient list. Then we realised steak was rather expensive and Bella wouldn't let me dry strips in the airing cupboard.'

The cookery teacher, handing back the critic's food, gawped.

'Didn't want anything dripping on the towels,' explained Bella.

'So,' continued Robert, 'we thought fundamentally, it's flat dry beef isn't it? So we seasoned some mince, squashed it between some greaseproof and dried it out in the oven. Maybe next time we'll take it out a little earlier.'

The critic held it down with the flat of his knife and inveigled the tines of the fork into it. Failing to cut a slice, he lifted the whole disc and nibbled round the edges.

'Certainly dry,' he said, after three minutes' chewing, 'definite smoky taste.'

'That's the one which caught on fire I think,' said Bella.

'That was the appetiser,' said Robert, 'now for the starter.'

'I think I'd better get that,' said Bella, 'you clear the plates.'

Robert stacked the dishes, picking at the leftovers and followed Bella out of the room. The critic sniffed at the jug of water and sighed.

'Thought it might be gin,' he said, 'when do you suppose we get wine?'

'We're teetotal,' said Robert, coming back in with a basket of bread rolls, 'we gave up strong drink years ago. Well I did. My daughters seem to offer Bella wine whenever they see her.'

'I'm not surprised,' muttered the critic.

Bella entered with bowls of soup.

'Caldo Verde com explosão!' said Robert.

'Er…' said the blogger, 'when you say explosio … is it safe?'

'Oh it's just a play on words,' Robert explained, 'the recipe is a traditional Portuguese speciality. Only we don't like spicy food very much, so we've substituted the chouriço with Cumberland bangers. I didn't know the Portuguese for banger, but explosão seemed to cover it! Humph.'

The diners relaxed a little, poking about and fishing out wheels of curled sausage which slithered off their spoons and splashed into the soup. The critic wiped a piece of cabbage from his shirt, poured more water and sighed. The blogger took something from her bag and took a sip.

'Flower remedy,' she said to the others' raised eyebrows.

'I use that for when I teach 4B,' said the teacher, looking at the little bottle hopefully.

The blogger handed it over.

'And now for the main event!' announced Robert.

Bella struggled in with a huge tureen.

'Our eldest daughter sent us one of her favourite recipes and here it is!'

Robert opened his mouth and above the strains of 'Donald where's your troosers' coming from the CD player he started some ear-shrivelling singing:

'"Jambalaya, codfish-eyes, cherry crumble!"'

'What all of them?' interrupted the teacher as he started making up the next line.

Robert closed his mouth and recovered himself.

'No, just jambalaya. Laura says I've got the lyrics wrong and to look it up on the internet. She's no fun sometimes. Don't know what's wrong with just buying a song-book. Maybe I'll do that. You can never have enough books.'

He looked round at his empty room and sighed. Bronwen, watching from behind the cameras thought of the bowed bookcases and boggled.

'So anyway, Laura's recipe was a bit on the spicy side too, so we adapted it and brought in a Scots element in honour of Bella's parents.'

The critic peered at the plate of sludge being dished up in front of him. He started to enumerate the ingredients while the blogger took more notes.

'OK,' he said, 'rice, chicken (I think), celery, onions, tomatoes … what are these?'

'Well those are the bits we tweaked,' said Robert, 'we don't like spicy sausage and sweet peppers can be, shall we say, anti-social. We used haggis and neeps instead.'

'Neeps?'

'Swede. Actually, it's turnip.'

'Only the haggis sort of exploded,' said Bella, 'and the neeps are a bit overcooked.'

The teacher closed her eyes, took a mouthful and waggled her head from side to side.

'Quite nice in a way reminiscent of a Louisiana swamp and Highland peat bog,' she said, 'you could call it McCajun.'

The food critic stared at her and tried to wrestle the flower remedy out of the blogger's hand.

Failing, he said 'I really could do with a drink. I probably don't want to know, but what's this "sock-blaster"? Please tell me it's not actually made with socks.'

'How could we forget!' said Robert.

As Bella cleared the places again, he brought in a bottle. Bronwen exchanged glances with Giles. It seemed that the contents of the jar had grown and clarified. A seething but clear golden liquid bubbled against the glass.

'Now *this* is a little spicy. It's home-brewed ginger beer. I don't *think* it's alcoholic. Do you want to open it or shall I?' said Robert.

'Perhaps we'll leave it for the moment,' said the critic, 'maybe after the dessert. I see you've made a spelling error. It should be Guinness Cake, shouldn't it?'

'Well, that's what the recipe was. It's got an old family story behind it.'

'I thought you were teetotal,' said the teacher, reaching for the bottle of golden liquid and then withdrawing her hand.

'We are, so I didn't make it with Guinness. I made it with cola. It turned out less of a cake and more sort of zabaglione with heart.'

Bella placed three dishes in front of their guests. A dark brown froth billowed.

Each of them tipped their spoons in and took a taste of the foam. It was quite pleasant, very sweet with an underlying taste of nutmeg and cinnamon. They relaxed. The teacher went in for a deeper mouthful. Her spoon hit something solid which shot out of the bowl, slammed into the bottle then bounced back into her lap.

For a few seconds, the bottle shuddered and the diners watched it, their spoons suspended. Bubbles started to gather in the bottom and increase. They rose to the top and frothed against the bottom of the cork and then, with the cameras still rolling, the bottle exploded.

*****

TEXTS

JANE: So have you got your posh frock for the award ceremony?
LAURA: Have I got to go?
JANE: Don't be so boring. You might get to meet that actor you fancy.
LAURA: Which would be great if I wasn't so embarrassed.
JANE: Could be worse.
LAURA: How?
JANE: Good point.
LAURA: I feel a bit sorry for that Bronwen. She wanted to be nominated in the documentary category.
JANE: There's probably more money in comedy. She'll get over it.
LAURA: We are never, ever going to live this down.
JANE: Meh. It's a free dinner.
LAURA: As long as Dad hasn't cooked it.
JANE: Funny you should say that…

Dad - The Hero

In the Dark

1973 Winter - I remember

There was a loud bang and all the lights in the house went out.

'Curses!' said Dad from the lean-to.

The bang had nothing to do with the darkness. Everyone's lights were out. I peered out of the dining room window and down the street. No lights. I peered out of the sitting room window across to the village on the mountain beyond the river. No lights.

Power cuts were so frequent in the winter of 1973, that Mum's main concern was that our supply of candles might not hold out. At the time. I wasn't entirely sure why it was all happening. There were a lot of angry people on the news blaming the government and the government was blaming the angry people. And the grown-ups didn't seem to realise how much fun it all was, apart from Dad.

'At least we've got a gas cooker,' said Mum bringing dinner in and putting it on the table, 'think of all those poor people with electric cookers.'

We'd brought the table into the sitting room. Without central heating, the dining room was freezing and there was no point in an electric heater if the power was off more than it was on. But coal burning in the fire warmed the sitting-room.

'After dinner, if the electric doesn't come back, can we play Monopoly?' I said.

'I hate Mopopoly,' came Jane's voice from under the table.

'We'll play "Contraband",' said Mum, 'no-one has to try and read anything much.'

'You've got to see how much the duty is,' I said.

'We can guess.'

'Huh,' came Jane's voice.

'Get up Jane,' said Mum, then she called, 'come on Robert, dinner's going cold.'

Dad came in with a candle on a saucer. Its yellow light flickered in the draught from the window and made the cottage pie look mysterious and exotic.

'The wine's exploded again,' he said.

'You and your wine,' sighed Mum.

Dad's latest hobby was brewing. He'd started with beer, filling the kitchen with the smell of hops and barley, giving us spoonfuls of malt to lick before tipping the rest into the roiling mass. The alchemy of brewing was fascinating. All those wonderful words: demijohn, grommet, syphon, bubbler, airlock. I could have sat for ages watching the bubbles gloop in the airlock.

After a while, he'd decided he preferred beer in a pub and moved on to wine. He tried shop bought kits but decided that the standard wasn't high enough.

'I need a book,' he'd said. Naturally.

'You can make wine out of anything!' he'd said, starting with wine made from tea leaves. I wondered if Mum had told her Ayrshire aunts.

They don't make great aunts like they used to. Nowadays they dish out money and treats. The ones I had all seemed to have gone to a training school to teach them how to stop children from getting uppity. Generally the married ones were scary and the maiden ones (whose career options hadn't been blighted by husbands and children) were good fun, if old fashioned. But the two elderly sisters on the west coast of Scotland, while very kind, had stopped the clock somewhere around 1920 in what would have been their teenage years. They had been shaped by rigid Presbyterian disapproval. Dad utterly baffled them.

One summer two years earlier, in preparation for a day of freezing in the sea-filled open air pool at Troon, Dad had been teaching us to swim by getting us to lie on foot-stools in the aunts' sitting-room and do the breast-stroke. It was rather exhausting for him.

'I'd quite like a glass of sherry before lunch, have you any?' he'd asked.

'We keep it for medicinal purposes only,' said Great Aunt B, 'we wouldn't *ever* drink it for pleasure.'

'I would,' said Dad, 'and the children can have a sip too.'

'But they're four and seven!'

'The French do it, why not us?' he'd argued.

The Great Aunts narrowed their lips on their views of the French. One of whom had snared their eldest brother during WW1 so that afterwards he'd moved abroad to marry her and never come back. Then they'd lost their younger brother, my grandfather, to England.

Jane and I jumped off the foot-stools and headed off into the garden.

'Yes, but the girls are hoydens already,' said Great Aunt T, following us, 'what are they doing now?'

'They're fine,' Dad had said, as Jane and I played cowboys and Indians in the garden. I tied her to the post of the washing line and circled her, waving the peg basket with menace and muttering threats.

'Let me go!!!!' shrieked Jane. She was grinning.

'They're not very lady-like,' complained Great Aunt B.

'Say "please" Jane,' called Dad.

'Let me go please!!!!' yelled Jane.

'You see,' Dad had said, 'perfect manners. Now where's that sherry? And is it that lovely soup for lunch?'

Anyway, so somehow I doubted anyone had told them that not only was he brewing his own wine, but letting his children try it. Not that in general we liked the taste.

'What are you making this one out of Dad?' I said.

'Raisins. Well it was supposed to be raisins, but I used mixed dried fruit with citrus peel and glacé cherries instead. It was all we had in the cupboard. I'm sure it'll be fine when it stops exploding.'

'Yuk,' said Jane.

'What's Jane doing under the table?' said Dad.

'Sulking,' I said.

'Well she can't. Get out from under the table Jane and sit up properly,' he peered under to try and see where she was. I knew where she was because she was punching my legs. But even Jane knew it was pointless arguing with Dad. She clambered out and flumped down on her chair and put her head down on the table.

'Elbows off the table,' said Dad.

'What's the matter Jane?' said Mum.

'She's not gonna,' said Jane, 'I'm not gonna let her.'

'"She's not going to",' said Dad, 'and "I'm not going to let her". Who's not going to do what?'

'Laura's not going to teach me.'

'I don't want to anyway,' I said through a mouthful of cottage pie.

'Don't eat with your mouth full,' said Dad, 'teach you what?'

Jane started to eat and said nothing. I could see her eyes glistening in the candle-light.

'Her teacher wants me to teach her to read,' I said, 'she gave me some flash cards.'

I wasn't sure which one of us was more mortified. I had been hauled out of my classroom nine and sent to Jane's. In front of the class, Jane's teacher had said, 'now Laura, I hear you're good at English but your sister doesn't seem to want to learn to read,' one of the other children sniggered, 'so I thought perhaps you could help at home and teach her these words over the weekend. They're very simple.'

None of us knew why Jane was finding reading so hard. She loved books. She loved stories. Our parents read to us, I read to her. Mum worried it was her fault. She had taught me to read before starting school but then educational theories changed and she'd been told not to 'confuse' Jane by interfering with the way the school would teach her when she was five. But it turned out that words were nonsense to Jane. She knew all her numbers, but letters were just wobbly confusing shapes which wanted to trip her up.

Today, we'd got home from school and I'd shown her one card with the word 'bed' written on it and after a moment's thought Jane had said 'deb'.

'No,' I'd said, 'try again.'

She looked at it a second time, 'peb' she'd said.

'No, it's…'

She had snatched the card from my hand and ripped it in two, then burst into tears.

Now over dinner, I said 'I can't Dad, I don't know how. And it's not fair anyway. And Miss Brown was mean to do that to Jane in front of the whole class.'

Jane rubbed her eyes with the back of her hand.

'Miss Brown says I'm thick,' said Jane.

I put my arm round her. 'You're not thick,' I said.

'You call me stupid sometimes,' she sniffed.

'Well,' I pointed out, 'that's because you're my little sister. But you're not really stupid, you're not.'

It was true, she wasn't. She was funnier than me, she was better at making (and keeping) friends than me, she was braver than me. If someone bullied me, I cried because I thought it might make them ashamed. If someone bullied Jane, she'd just hit them. In fact she'd have hit anyone who bullied me if my pride would have let her. She was faster and better at climbing. She could balance on a bike better and she could roller-skate which I couldn't do at all. She just couldn't read. She looked at the words and either couldn't decipher them at all or read them backwards or she muddled the letters into the wrong order.

'Mmm,' said Dad, 'well you won't learn to read if you don't eat your dinner. And afterwards, I'll have a think. This might be a job for Boanerges.'

By the time we'd finished dinner, Jane had cheered up a little. The power was still off, so we played "Contraband". The card game involved taking it in turns to be travellers smuggling items through customs or the official trying to stop them. It was great fun, as we tried to guess who was lying. Did Mum really have nothing to declare? Who had the silk stockings? Who had the whisky? Most importantly who had the Ruritanian Crown Jewels? And when Jane said she had the diplomatic bag, was she telling the truth?

The cards with their 1950s sketches were beautiful. It was hard to look at the silk stockings and imagine them so valuable you might want to smuggle them. Mum's tights never looked worth anything. In the candle-light, it was hard to read the duty on the game's tiny slip of paper so half the time we made it up.

Dad went into full interrogation mode as customs officer. He waggled his eyebrows, dropped his voice and leaned forward, 'are you telling me the trooooooth little girl?' and wiggled his ears so his glasses moved. Keeping a straight face was only possible by putting all my tension into my toes, crunched up out of sight.

When he was a possible smuggler, he was cherubic with innocence. 'I just have to pay duty on some silk stockings,' he quavered, 'they're not for me of course,' (little giggle), 'they're for my beautiful wife.'

'No diamond watch?'

'Certainly not!'

'No Crown Jewels?'

'Indeed no. I am but a lowly man…'

He almost always got away with it.

After a few rounds, the lights came back on. Jane and I went out to do the washing up. We usually argued over this but she seemed so fed-up I did the drying up, which was the chore we both hated most.

Mum was folding down the table and talking to Dad who had gone into the study.

'What's dyslexia?' she said.

'I don't know much about it,' said Dad's muffled voice, 'it's sometimes called word blindness. Some educationalists think it's an indication of ability, others think there's something else going on.'

'See,' said Jane, putting her thumb in her mouth and going to put the TV on, 'I'm thick.'

Dad was still talking, 'I think the educational theory is to keep on at the child until it learns out of fear.'

I recognised that method. It had worked with me and times tables. I wasn't sure it was going to work with Jane and words.

'I think,' said Dad, emerging with some paper and pens, 'they're barking up the wrong tree. For a start, those reading books are terrible.'

'Laura managed,' said Mum. Jane hunched in her chair and stared at the divers on 'Jacques Cousteau'.

'Laura would read a bus ticket if there was nothing else available,' said Dad, 'it's the way she is. Jane is different. Not worse, not better. Just different. But even Laura found those books boring didn't you Laura?'

It had been a while since I'd read a book I hadn't taken into school myself. I cast my mind back to 'Janet and John' and 'Peter and Jane'. They were impossibly old fashioned even by my standards. Although secretly I longed for the girls' frilly dresses and curly hair, I didn't envy their lifestyle which seemed to involve an endless round of dolls' tea-parties and 'helping Mummy' with the housework. John and Peter occasionally helped Daddy mend a car or repair a bike, but mostly they were out in the wilds making dens and sailing boats.

'Yes,' I said. I had long since moved through 'The Famous Five' and Henry Treece and was now starting on Alan Garner's mysteries where worlds collided and crossed.

'What Jane needs is cheering up!' said Dad, 'you can't learn when you're miserable. Let's see those flash cards.'

I got them out of my satchel and handed them over.

Dad shuffled them and held one up with the word 'bad' written on it.

'Dab?' said Jane, 'pad? Dap? Apd? Dba?' Her lip wobbled.

'Mmm,' said Dad, turning the card over and looking at it, 'I think I can see why you're finding it hard.'

'Can you?'

'Yes, your eyes are seeing the letters and then something is turning them upside down or backwards. You *can* read, Jane. It's just that your brain is panicking and we need to get it to calm down. Remember Eric Morcambe on the piano? "I'm playing all the right notes, but not necessarily in the right order"? That's what you're doing with letters. Don't worry, everything will be fine. Once you start having fun, there'll be no stopping you. Give me a few hours and tomorrow, Boanerges will be in action.'

'Boanerges won't be in action tonight though will he?' said Jane.

'Not tonight.'

'Phew.'

Dad sat down and started to write on his paper. I went into the study to find the notebook I wrote poems in. Dad had 'borrowed' it to read and not given it back. The bathroom was now upstairs in what had once been the second biggest bedroom. The study was what had been the bathroom at the beginning of the year. We'd moved most of the books into the study and they lined the wall on sagging shelves.

At the far end of the room was the desk. It had been Mum's grandfather's and had somehow survived several moves and Dad. There were keyholes on all the drawers, but the keys themselves were long lost and it wasn't possible to lock anything away. It was a shame. There is nothing as mysterious as a locked drawer. I always hoped I'd find a secret catch in it somewhere, but so far, I'd had no luck.

On top of the desk was Boanerges. He was a typewriter. Definitely male. Very old. Roughly as portable as a hippopotamus who had swallowed granite. It was only Dad who had the requisite strength to make the keys move with any kind of fluidity. The typewriter was called Boanerges which means 'sons of thunder' because of the noise made when you typed anything. This was why Jane was relieved about the fact he wasn't going to be used after she'd gone to bed. She slept above the study.

I looked around for my note-book but it was a fairly impossible task. As Dad had suggested, every time we had guests, the general chaos was shoved into the study. Not just that, but we had more books than book shelves and Dad had recently decided to buy the Encyclopaedia Britannica by instalments. I gave up and went back to finish watching Jacques Cousteau exploring rusty ancient artefacts in clear tropical seas.

'Bed time!' said Dad when it finished, 'busy day tomorrow. Chop, chop, I'll be up in a bit!' He was too intent on his writing to look up.

Jane and I went upstairs, undressed and brushed our teeth. We'd go into Jane's room first where Dad would come to read the next chapter of 'Watership Down'. We were struggling to follow the plot but were absorbed by the atmosphere: the dark warmth of the burrow, the bloody battles, Fiver's terrifying visions. After that, I'd be reading 'The Owl Service' under the covers with a torch. It was getting to an exciting bit.

'Do you really think I'm not stupid?' said Jane, as we cuddled under the quilt.

'You're my little sister, of course you're stupid,' I said, 'but you're not stupid the way you think you are.'

'Do you think Dad can help me learn to read?'

'Dad can do anything.'

'Except tidy up.'

'Except tidy up.'

'And cook Spanish omelette without burning the bottom.'

'Yeah.'

'And sing.'

'Doesn't stop him trying though.'

She giggled through her thumb and twiddled my hair.

'It'll be ok,' I said, 'Dad'll work it out.'

Dad came up a few moments later and sat on Jane's chair. He didn't have 'Watership Down' but his sheets of paper covered in his scrawling capitals and line drawings. We leaned forward but he pulled it back to his chest until we sat back.

'"Miss Myfanwy Price was a squirrel who kept a general store in a forest in South Wales."' he started. '"She sold tooth strengthener to the squirrels, strong gloves to the moles, corn pockets to the mice and parachutes for baby birds. One day, as she was hanging up her washing in the attic, a shadow fell across her, and to her surprise the scruffiest eagle she had ever seen, landed on the branch beside her. 'Have you got anything to keep my feathers tidy, Miss Price?' said the eagle. Miss Myfanwy Price was very frightened. She had heard that eagles <u>ate</u> squirrels, and this one was <u>very</u> big indeed."'

He stopped and showed us his drawing of Myfanwy staring up at an eagle as she stood next to a rotary washing line.

Jane pulled her thumb out of her mouth, 'What happens next Daddy?' she said.

'Ah,' said Dad, folding up his story and opening 'Watership Down' instead, 'I'm going to type this up first thing tomorrow. Then we'll go shopping and go to the Kardomah for something to eat. If you want to know whether Myfanwy gets eaten, you'll have to sit with me while we have lunch and help me read it. And when you have worked out some of the words, just some of them, we'll have knickerbocker glories to celebrate! And maybe you can give me some ideas for more Myfanwy stories (if she doesn't get eaten that is). It'll take us a while to start with I expect, but we'll get there in the end. You'll be reading before you know it Jane, and once you start, you'll be as bad as Laura.'

Probably Dad used all the wrong techniques, probably he should have researched phonics or something. But it didn't matter. It took a while but with Myfanwy's help and some pestering at the school, he got Jane reading because he had faith in her. One day, the letters made sense and she could read and she hasn't looked back since.

Sometimes the faith that everything will one day make sense is all anyone needs to keep going.

Taking a Break

2012 Thursday

We are all fidgety. The morning, before we are allowed to visit intensive care, drags. I come back from shopping to find that Jane, having given up tidying the third bedroom which is full of mainly craft supplies and has started dusting one of the smaller bookcases.

She is sitting on the floor with the complete set of hardcover Narnia books, the ones Dad had read to them over and over again.

'Do you remember, do you remember?'

Outside, the sun shines, a proper June day. We drink coffee and look out of the sitting room window down towards the silvery line which is the not so distant sea, sparkling and twinkling, undefined but beautiful.

At the hospital, Dad is quiet. He breathes in and he breathes out. He does not move very much.

There is nothing much to talk about any more.

'Do you remember the Kardomah? says Jane, 'I used to love watching the coffee grinders and smelling the fresh beans and seeing the machines bubbling away. There weren't many proper coffee shops back then were there?'

'It's still there,' says Mum, stroking Dad's hand, 'we go sometimes, don't we Robert?'

'Do you remember the knickerbocker glories?' I say, 'they were massive. All that cream and ice-cream and jelly and chopped fruit.'

'We never could finish them could we?' says Jane, 'Dad always had to do it for us. Not that he ever minded.'

'I know but it was such a treat. Knickerbocker glories are the most exciting thing that could ever happen in a coffee shop.'

We look at Dad, peaceful, still beyond our reach, still breathing in and out, in and out, the machines still embroidering their coloured lines with a steady bleep bleep bleep.

Coffee at Tiffany's

Tiffany had thought they'd be trouble when they first came in.
She'd nearly called her mum. But then she thought, *if I want to
prove I can run a place like this, I've got to learn to handle this
sort of thing.*

It was the electric scooter that caused the first bit of difficulty. By the time the old duffer had nearly demolished the café's door-frame and Tiffany and the old dear had reorganised half the tables to let him through and he'd told her to tell her mum to get a ramp from Argos, she nearly needed a coffee herself. But he'd been very polite about it all and lifted his hat in her direction. Tiffany didn't know why. His head looked like it could do with all the covering it could get as his hair had long since given up the ghost. But it seemed like a nice gesture whatever it was for.

Now twice a week, there he sat like a king, contemplating the menu he knew off by heart and stroking his beard. He looked like a scrawny Father Christmas since he'd been on a diet. Tiffany knew he was dieting because he told her his progress (pound by pound) every time he came in. His wife was a sweetie too, although rather quiet. She hadn't much choice since Old Mr D was always wittering on to her; reading stuff out of the paper or taking photos of her on his phone when she ate anything messy. He'd then text them off to someone and read the reply to Mrs D. In Tiffany's general opinion, old people shouldn't be allowed mobiles: they left them behind, forgot to turn them on, didn't charge them up and took four hundred years to do a text. But she had to hand it to Mr D. He was a pretty good at it. Meanwhile his wife quietly ate her snack and gazed into space. Tiffany hoped Mrs D never got cross-examined on anything Mr D was saying; she was pretty sure that Mrs D was a lot more interested in her day-dream.

All in all, she'd sort of got quite fond of them, even though Mr D kept calling her Tamara or Tabitha and once, for no apparent reason Meredith.

One day, when it was really busy, Mr D folded the local paper, gave their order and then started talking about his children. Boggling a bit, Tiffany wondered briefly if he had a younger woman somewhere as Mrs D was clearly well past it. There was a horrible few seconds when she wondered if he was still doing *that* at his age before she shook the image away and asked how old their daughters were.

Mr D looked round the crowded café and nodded in the general direction of about three tables. 'Girls like those two,' he said.

Tiffany considered the customers in question. Apart from another ancient couple of pensioners there was a teenage mother with toddler daughter (and the mess Tiffany would have to clear up later) and two women gossiping over a hot chocolate with extra cream and a pot of English Breakfast tea for one. The thought that Mr D had a toddler at his age was too awful to contemplate so Tiffany asked hopefully, 'do you mean the two ladies with the nice big handbags?'

'That's right' Mrs D answered, 'although they'll put their backs out if they're not careful. And they ought to start growing old gracefully rather than dying their hair red.'

'Just like our girls,' Mr D sighed, 'and the same silly clothes. They dress as if they were young girls like you even though they're in their thirties. Or is it forties, Laura? Let's see, how old am I?'

While the arithmetic got under way, Tiffany gawped at the two middle-aged women and considered exactly how much they *weren't* dressed like her. If anyone made *her* wear those clothes she'd never leave the house.

'Forty-six next week? Really?' Mr D exclaimed, 'Tabitha, what should we get her? We never get it right. What do young women want these days?'

'Er' hesitated Tiffany, with no idea what someone her mother's age would want except for 'some peace and quiet, some respect and five minutes to myself without someone demanding something', which was all Mum ever droned on about. 'What artist is she into?'

'I'm not sure, Monet perhaps?'

'Don't know them, what have they done?'

'The Waterlilies?'

'Sounds nice. Don't know it thought, is it Indie, House, Acid, (no, too old probably), Punk?'

The old couple and Tiffany stared at each other across the chasm of sixty years. Luckily Mum came up just then and the question was put to her.

'Has she got kids of her own?' asked Tiffany's mum and getting an affirmative reply, declared predictably: 'If it was me, I'd want some peace and quiet, some respect and five minutes to myself without someone demanding something.'

Tiffany rolled her eyes.

'What about some nice underwear?' Tiffany's mum suggested.

'I'd never get the right sort,' Mrs D replied sadly, 'she won't wear sensible knickers at all. I can't believe she doesn't get cold kidneys.'

There was no reply to this and Tiffany left them to it as she went on her rounds of the tables. The other old couple were having quite a beanfeast considering it wasn't pension day, but they weren't a bit polite like Mr & Mrs D.

'Gor, you're a bit slow aren't ya?' said the old geezer 'we asked for them éclairs ages ago, and top up our coffees will ya? – think we should get it for nuffink, we've had to wait so long.'

The old bat with him was considering the menu. Her flipping shopping trolley was right in the gangway but when Tiffany tried to move it slightly, the obnoxious cow slapped her hand and swore; as if Tiffany would have been seen dead with a tartan shopping trolley. Or indeed any colour shopping trolley.

Mr & Mrs D enveloped in the steam from their beverages and holding hands across the table, turned at the commotion and looked in outrage at the other couple.

'Wot you staring at granddad?' snarled the other old man.

'I apologise if I caused offence,' Mr D replied calmly, 'It's just that I don't think young Tamara meant any harm, she was only trying to make sure the gangway was DDA compliant, which as a fellow disabled man, you'd appreciate was essential.'

'Whatever,' said the other old woman, 'come on, let's pay up and get out.'

She chucked a ten pound note on the table and snapped 'keep the change, not that you deserve it' at Tiffany. Rising abruptly she started to manoeuvre her trolley, arm muscles straining under her cardi. The old man meanwhile snatched up his walking stick which had fallen to the floor and jumped to his feet. 'Yeah, let's get out of this dump but I'm not leaving a tenner.'

He grabbed at the money and started to rummage for loose change.

Mr and Mrs D suddenly caught each other's eyes and Mr D rapidly texted something. Mrs D's phone went off and she read it. With a barely noticeable nod at her husband, she rose (a little creakily) and then fell as if in a faint, across the top of the tartan shopping trolley. Just as the nasty old couple started to push her off, there was a loud whine and Tiffany got out of the way just in time as Mr D shot forwards with his electric scooter, pinning 'nasty old bat' against the table and parking his wheels firmly on top of the 'nasty old geezer's' feet. They were both trapped.

'Quick Tiffany, ring the police!!' shouted out Mrs D, 'It's the jewellery shop robbery gang from the paper! They're in disguise!'

*****

As the sirens faded into the distance, the inspector sat back with a cup of tea and stared at the unlikely detectives in front of him. Tiffany rushed up with a plate of cream cakes and some hot chocolate.

'What made you realise they weren't what they seemed?' he asked in amazement, 'their disguises were brilliant'

'The clothes and make-up, yes,' explained Mr D, '(you know you shouldn't let me eat these Tamara, you're undoing all the work I've put into my diet).'

'It was the way they acted,' continued Mrs D, while Mr D licked cream from his moustache, 'no-one our age could read a menu at that distance without reading glasses.'

'When that bogus pensioner arrived, he could barely walk even with his stick,' added Mr D, the crumbs from his doughnut trembling on his beard, 'but when he needed to, he moved like an oiled machine.'

'OMG!!!' exclaimed Tiffany, 'I'd never have noticed that. You're totally mint!'

'You shouldn't really say OMG, Tabitha dear,' Mr D gently reproved 'and anyway, it should be OFR'

'OFR?' Tiffany queried, 'I've never heard that one'

'It's simple,' Mr D declared triumphantly, 'Old Fogies Rule. OK??!'

Dad - The Wonderer

Like the First Morning

Christmas 1973 - I remember
It was Dad who had helped make church fun. He entered into the
spirit of plays and readings with a gusto which should have
earned him an Oscar. Exactly what he'd have got it for was
another matter.

But he also helped church make sense.

He was the one who bought me the book. On white pages, brightly coloured pictures were vivid. In the book, children were welcomed no matter their colour or gender or ability. In it, a man said 'if you have two coats and someone else has none, give him your spare coat.' In it was kindness and forgiveness and the chance to start again.

Dad was the one who stood next to me as sun slanted through the window and we sang 'Morning has broken' from a modern hymn-book whose cover was in my favourite colours: a swirl of blue and green and turquoise and teal.

He was the one, like me, struggling to keep still in a Quaker service, explaining the majesty of ancient cathedrals and the simplicity of our plain church, teaching me to respect other people's beliefs or lack of them, even when I didn't agree with them. Yes, he taught me to respect.

His childhood had not involved church a great deal, although he had devout Anglican and Methodist aunts and uncles. His own mother had a quiet faith, but his father was not interested. Mum's childhood has also not involved church a great deal, but she and Dad married in a Presbyterian church, very different from the one Mum's parents had rejected. So I grew up going to church most Sundays. Women as well as men preached in our church and I received my very own Bible on Palm Sunday. I stood in shafts of light singing and sat in peaceful quiet tuning in to the infinite. Dad taught me to appreciate those things.

When we moved to Wales, church was different. To start with, Dad tried to join the local chapels but they were very serious and mostly Welsh speaking. Women didn't even attend funerals. He found a church in Swansea and it was better. The building was freezing but the young people put on 'Godspell' and I was mesmerised by a faith which could be communicated in modern language. We once spent a whole Saturday preparing a costume so that Dad could play a Roman in church the next day. Mum sewed him a tunic out of an old sheet. Dad made himself a helmet and an eagle topped standard with SPQR on it and painted them in silver paint, the scent of the oil filling the sitting room.

In church, I learnt about forgiveness. Not just how to receive but the need to give. It was hard. Tina was bullying me. She had turned most of the class against me for no reason except she enjoyed it. School had become a torment and I was crying myself to sleep every night. I didn't want to forgive her.

But I did. And somehow, from that moment, I felt a little of the power shift to me. My heart was no longer full of hatred and I wasn't the one who felt pleasure in cruelty. That was something to be proud of.

And Dad taught me to find hope and peace in the beauty of ancient words and music as well as new ones.

Christmas 1973, as we would for several more years, we went back to Berkshire to stay at my grandparents' house and celebrate with Dad's wider family. Near midnight on Christmas Eve, we drove down winding lanes under star-sprinkled indigo skies and under trees which reach from either side to touch branches overhead. I had never been up so late on purpose.

We entered the tiny church where candlelight warmed the white plaster walls and the lead on stained glass windows.

The lecturn, where the Bible lay open, was in the form of the spreading wings of an eagle. Surrounded by flickering candles, the gold of its feathers appeared to ruffle ready for flight.

'"In the beginning was the Word…'

We were at the end of one year and in a few days a new one would begin.

An ending always brings a beginning.

But with faith and hope, things would, somehow, turn out all right.

Holding Hands

2012 Friday

I am beyond tired. I take off the eye mask I am wearing to cut out the light coming through the sitting room curtains and check my phone. It is 4am. I have been waking at this time for three days. There is no sound. It is the dead time of day, the time when nothing is awake, everything heavily asleep. Or dying. There is no sound from the bedroom, which means that either Mum and Jane have drifted into a snore-less sleep or more likely that they, like me, are awake and waiting.

For two hours I lie with my eyes closed, drifting in and out of sleep, reorganising and decluttering the bungalow in my head, a logistical problem with the nightmare element of Escher. There are two other bedrooms: one is full of office equipment, books, photos and dust and the other full: wall to wall, floor to ceiling with craft and boxes of fifty years of my parents' married life plus fifty years of my grandparents' married life and scattered throughout the house are even relics of my great and great-great grandparents. Jane and I have sorted and boxed all week but it's hardly made a dent.

At six, I get up. The easiest way to do this with minimum back pain, is to roll out of the z-bed onto the floor and get up from there. I fold up the bed and cuddle under the duvet on the sofa for a while and read. I will never be able to recall what I was reading: something meaningless and light probably. My mind is too fidgety for contemplation or meditation. At seven, I make everyone a cup of tea and have a bath. At eight, we are all sitting down to breakfast, table mats, teapot and everything. I ring home - James has a school trip and I am not there to make sure he has what he needs. Jane rings home too. There is nothing to say really. 'I love you, I miss you, I know, I know, thank you'.

We wash up and go to the supermarket. I decide I'll cook something nice for dinner tonight. The morning passes. What did we do with it? I will never remember.

For lunch we have sandwiches and Mum starts to say grace. And then she bursts into tears. 'I can't help it!' she cries out 'I love him so much.'

At the hospital, we sit for an age pressed against the bed. We have run out of things to say to Dad. He has become a bleep and a series of coloured lines of embroidery endlessly stitching themselves across a monitor. Numbers that mean nothing to me - good or bad - ascend and descend some scale of significance. Dad no longer even reacts to the hand stroking or our voices. He is deep within himself or gone, but Mum keeps gently urging him to wake up. After a while we are all silent. Jane falls asleep with her head on the side bar of the bed. I doze, realising after some time that the comfortable thing against my knee is a catheter bag and then not really caring. I look up at Mum and catch my breath. My seventy-four year old mother is bathed in light and looking intently into the wildly staring eyes oblivious to her. She looks younger than my earliest memories of her. She is seventy-four and her hair is white but in that moment she looks like a young girl, like an angel, in love, timeless.

After a while, we have to leave him for the consultants to consult over him. The waiting room for intensive care is like a sea with islands of misery. Families in various stages of hope and despair huddle in groups - no interaction, no catching of eyes, sleeping, staring into space, virtually silent.

And after another while, it is time to say goodbye. We sit with him, hand in hand, hand on soft beloved hand. The tubes are gone and the monitor is turned off so that it does not measure beat by slowing beat the progress between this life and the next adventure.

We read aloud to him, 'He will wipe every tear from their eyes. There will be no more death or mourning or crying or pain, for the old order of things has passed away.'

We wait.

Slipping Away

Dad…

He hears a voice but it is a long way away. He feels fingers on his hands and face but they too are distant, less than the feeling of a breeze on his skin. The weight of his discomfort and pain is lifting and suddenly he can no longer recall it. He hears words and he knows the words. They are dear to him. He would have known they were in his own tongue but now they are no longer words but a picture, an image coming into focus as the words fade away and become reality. The light dims and his eyes close. And his eyes open and he is away from pain, and weeping and suffering and the light will not diminish.

Dad – The Discombobulator

Starlight

1974 November - I remember

And then there was the time Dad threw a firework party.

In those days and where we lived, Hallowe'en wasn't much of a thing. If you wanted sweets pretty much for nothing, you waited for Christmas when you could go carol singing or, on 5th November, you made an effigy out of newspaper and old clothes and trailed round the houses demanding 'a penny for the guy'. At the end of the day, the guy would be put on top of a bonfire and set alight. Any vague sensitivities I might have had about the facts behind the tradition (I was that kind of child) were put aside for the sake of hard cash. Such was quite possibly the reality about the real Guy Fawkes's fate too. We preferred actual sweets but even a penny wasn't to be sniffed at since you could still get a quarter of sherbet from the post-office shop for about 10p. Or maybe you couldn't. It's a long time ago.

This was the year when Mum handed over with suspicious dexterity, Dad's most disreputable jumper and trousers to dress the guy. We made the guy a head out of a paper bag and were disappointed that Mum wouldn't hand over one of Dad's hats. But Mum was wise. Dad would have spotted the hat whereas he couldn't be sure about the clothes.

The good thing about bonfire night is that it's in November. By the time we were hoisting the guy onto the bonfire, it was dark. Dad, squinting at its attire with a slight frown, dismissed the thought that his own wife could be so duplicitous as to sacrifice his favourite tramp dressing-up outfit. Shaking the idea out of his head, he turned to plan the firework display.

The guests were, as far as I recall, Dad's colleagues from the office. What they made of the ascent to our road, with its double hair-pin bend I've no idea. So, it was November and it was dark and spitting with rain. The bonfire blazed, consuming the guy in Dad's oldest clothes. Jane and I wrote our names in the air with sparklers.

We all stood around in the damp cold watching Dad and a friend light fireworks.

Every time Dad lit the blue touch-paper, we tensed in case nothing happened. Then there was a soft fzz, a brief silence followed by a gentle sizzle and a few sparks which turned into a roar and cascade of colour: Roman candles, flares and fountains spat golds and reds and greens in every direction.

Then the rockets, fired into the starless night, higher than the roofs, higher than the mountain, exploding above our heads and cascading in shreds of silver and gold, spiralling down and down and melting into nothing.

'Last but not least, the Catherine wheel!' said Dad. He nailed it to a fence post and lit the paper. But by now the spitting rain had passed through a bad tempered drizzle and was starting to drench into everyone's clothes.

'Inside the garage!' said Dad.

The garage was huge. There was room for two cars but it had never housed any or at least none of ours. Half of it was a heavy duty version of indoors without the books.

Dad nailed the catherine wheel to a random piece of wood and positioned it upright using the vice on his workbench.

He relit the fuse.

Again, there was the fzz and the pause and then with the fury of a small dragon who's trapped his tail in a revolving door, the Catherine wheel started to spin and spit sparks. For a couple of minutes, it lit up the open mouthed faces of the watchers. It lit up the lawnmower and the garden tools and the plant pots and the empty jars. It lit up bicycles, roller skates, the discarded doll's pram and Mum's 1950s ice-skates and snow shoes. It lit up the lathe, a straw archery butt, some old packing cases with newspaper in, the half finished wooden-dolls-house, the half-finished doll's cradle, the cat basket and the abandoned ant farm.

Then the garage filled with thick, black smoke.

Coughing and scrambling, the blinded guests helped each other outside into the early stages of a downpour.

'It's fine,' called Dad, 'it's gone out now!'

'The thing about Robert,' choked out one of his colleagues, 'he's either mad or a genius.'

'He might be both,' coughed the other, 'but either way, he's unforgettable.'

Still in Charge

2012

The hearse has pulled up to the house. Everyone is there except Uncle David and Aunt Lily. A frantic phone call. They're lost. Somewhere nearby, bamboozled by Welsh road-signs, they have pulled over to be rescued.

I run with my husband run past the hearse and drive off to find them. I get my phone out to text 'Dad - you'll never guess...' and then remember. My eyes fill, but I chuckle all the same.

He would have loved this. Late for his own funeral. No-one's going to organise Dad if he doesn't want them to.

In the Mansion

'Well that's all a bit gloomy,' says Robert, 'they need to cheer up.'

He is rummaging round trying to find his latest magnum opus. Stuff is piled up everywhere and it is already chaos. The angel appears to stand still but it's using its wings to tidy things up a little. They can do that you know. The angel is wondering how it's possible to make a heavenly mansion look untidy. Not only has Robert managed this but has also somehow found a celestial pile of books and made them dusty.

Robert pauses, 'they'll be all right won't they?'

The angel nods and smiles, 'they have each other and they have love and faith.'

Robert stretches his limbs without pain and in triumph holds aloft his manuscript. Its plot and theme are impossible to describe.

'Laura always said I should write what I knew about,' he says with a smirk, 'wait till she reads this.'

After a few moments scribbling and frowning at the angel's attempts to organise his clouds, Robert casts aside his work.

'Do you know what?' he says to the angel, 'one of the best things about heaven is that I can sing. Really sing. No tone-deafness, no out of key-ness. I can sing. So I'm going to.'

The angel tenses. This could go one way or another. There are ageless hymns and there is the 1952 YHA songbook. Robert limbers up and opens his mouth:

'There once was a spirit called Angel Finnegan

'Grew some whiskers on his chinnegan

'Wind came out and blew them in again

'Poor old Angel Finnegan, begin again

'There once was a spirit called...'

The angel's worst fears are realised. I bet you didn't know angel could wince, did you?

A Fine Mess

Clearing out a wardrobe in middle years is an exploration of hope over reality. I wish I was tidy. I quite enjoy the catharsis of taking a massive bag of clothes and books to the charity shop. I take pleasure in polishing when there's a clear surface to dust. But I really wish someone else could magic away the clutter.

This suit, yes it made me look elegant and corporate but…. I bought it eleven years ago and haven't been able to fit into it for eight. Why is it still there?

And the lovely party dress bought on a whim online. In the wrong size. There it hangs, six years later, forlorn and unworn waiting for me to regain my once elfin figure and for a party invitation when I can get into it.

At the bottom of the wardrobe was my dissertation, unread since it was handed in. The cover is stained from where it got damp once. It was rescued when I cleared out my parents' shed in 2013. I try to visualise the earnest young woman stabbing away at a typewriter. She is long gone, but I can remember the agony of producing every word, even though most of them now make no sense, since the average goldfish bowl is more profound. Back in the wardrobe it goes, because the only other place to put it is an overloaded bookcase.

Somewhere in my system there must be at least one tidy gene. Unfortunately, it has been mislaid in the chaos of all the untidy ones. I like a neat working environment for writing, drawing or sewing. If necessary, I will turn my back on anything out of place elsewhere in the room (I'd never do anything creative otherwise) and for example can write in my little writing corner while behind me are four piles of clean laundry.

The plus side of having been brought up in a house where a clear worktop was just wasted space is that I can cook in an area the size of a side-plate if necessary; a skill which makes me able to cope with the catering side of camping with nonchalance.

Personally, I blame my parents. One of my earliest
memories is one of a room, floor to ceiling (or at least above my
three year old head) with stuff. I can't now recall what stuff
although books featured significantly. However, I do remember a
glass case with a stuffed red squirrel inside. It had fascinating
shiny eyes. There was also a musical box which had real
butterflies pinned to little rods which danced up and down when
the music played. They were very pretty, but I was sad that
something so free should be fixed so permanently. 'Are they
dead?' I asked. 'Afraid so but just as well.' Dad answered.
Sometime between then and when we moved to the next house,
both the squirrel and the musical box were sold. They had come
with my parents from their first home, a flat in Hendon which had
previously belonged to my father's aunt (who conveniently died
sometime before the wedding). As far as I can gather, my father
thus accumulated a number of her books (which covered a range
of the early 20th Century equivalent of New Agism, e.g.
Theosophy, British Israelitism and so on) and several odd items
she had either inherited or collected, including dead animals in
cases. Recently, friends took us to find that flat where my parents
started their married life and where I lived until I was eighteen
months old. It is fundamentally a maisonette created when a
house was split in two horizontally. At the time when I was born,
my parents lived in the top floor and one of my father's other
aunts lived on the ground floor. I took some exterior photographs
to show my mother and then did an internet search and discovered
interior shots from the last time it was sold.

'The bathroom looks a bit different,' said my mother in
some surprise, slightly affronted that it hadn't remained the same
for fifty years, 'and the sitting room never looked as roomy as
that when we were living there.'

'That's possibly because it's tidy now,' I pointed out.

'You might be right,' conceded Mum.

After moving from Hendon, we moved to Dunstable, then to Wokingham, then to Winnersh then to Aberdulais in South Wales. This was all in a space of seven years. If the proverbial rolling stone gathers moss, my rolling father gathered stuff. There is no other word for it unless you know a collective noun that covers books, half finished projects, paperwork which is in no order whatsoever and may have become irrelevant twenty years earlier, items inherited or handed down by relations who presumably didn't want them and knew my father was a sucker for that sort of thing, random bits of china and souvenirs etc etc. Stuff. What we had most of was books of course, thousands of them. When we moved to the house in Wales, we put the majority of them up in the front room on bowed bookshelves. Some of the villagers were incredulous. 'What they want all them books for?' they said, as if this was stranger than keeping baby alligators, which was what the adjoining neighbours did in *their* front room.

Eventually, my father and another neighbour moved the bathroom from downstairs into a bedroom upstairs and what had once been the bathroom became what we called the study. Only my father was capable of 'studying' in there. Everyone else was in fear of being crushed to death by something falling off the tottering piles of books and papers. Whenever my sister or I had a birthday party, or some masochistic relation came to stay, there was a frantic shoving of clutter into the study. If you subsequently wanted anything, it was an exercise similar to finding a specific geological strata in a range of mountains and probably more dangerous. After my ninth birthday party, the bully at school made nasty comments about our disordered house which made me hate it; but on the other hand, another friend a few years ago, a girl who came round regularly (not just when we'd shovelled a room clear) told me how refreshing it had been to visit a home where you could paint, sew, write, cook and no-one cared about the resulting chaos.

Incidentally, the study finally became too constricting even for my father to write in, so, after trying to work in the attic but finding it too dark, he constructed a room within the airing cupboard where he could put his electric typewriter and eventually a computer. Really, you've just got to believe me on this.

It's hard to imagine how my father turned out this way. Or maybe it was a natural reaction. My paternal grandmother was the archetypal housewife and kept her home streamlined and immaculate. My paternal grandfather was a prototype minimalist and couldn't bear mess or pictures at an angle or things on windowsills or dust or crumbs. He didn't show any evidence that small children playing caused him any pain, but we did have to tidy up after ourselves, which we virtually never did at home. My grandmother kept some decorative, feminine, pretty ornaments in her room where they wouldn't annoy my grandfather, but they were still kept very neat.

What my mother's excuse is, I have no idea. My maternal grandfather died before I was born but my maternal grandmother also kept a tidy, if arty, house and she too made sure my sister and I cleaned up after ourselves when we stayed. A recent TV programme showed young girls in the 1940s and 50s being chained to the home, training up as housewives. My mother just laughed. 'Never happened to me!' she said cheerfully.

So I assume that my mother had either not picked up any wifey skills before her marriage at twenty-three or lost interest in the face of my father's consequent refusal to do anything except hoard and live in chaos. Possibly a combination of both. He wasn't a man to be argued with, and I speak as one who tried. Dad regarded any sort of tidying, cataloging, organising or (heaven forbid) reducing the volume of stuff as a dark art.

When I mentioned the fact that I was doing my biennial book sort, culling the ones I didn't want and putting the remainder back into some sort of order by genre and author, he visibly shuddered, as if I was describing the slaughter of kittens with a pickaxe. Mum did try. She once took a mass of long unread science fiction books to a charity shop only for my father to buy them back a week later because 'I seem to have lost the ones I thought I had.'

She didn't pass on many home-making skills to me or my sister either. Both of us regard housework as a sort of Sisyphean task which has been set to punish us for something. On the other hand, Mum and Dad between them showed us how to be creative. There were story competitions and painting and papier-mâché and lino cutting. Every holiday Dad would try out some new craft with varying success: corn dollies, soap carving, pottery. There just wasn't much time for nonsense like dusting or vacuuming.

Long long after my sister and I had left home, my parents finally moved from the family home and into a bungalow, manfully trying to force nearly forty years of stuff into somewhere half the size of the place they were leaving and pretty nearly managing it, if you didn't mind the fact that there wasn't much floor. Recently, the old family home came up on the market and we looked in astonishment at the interior shots on the estate agent's website. It was impossible to recognise anything, including my old room, where latter owners had put a spiral staircase in the (creepy) corner into the attic which was now a light filled spacious room rather than a dark glory hole reminiscent of a junk shop.

In 2012, when my sister and I stayed for the last week of Dad's life as he lay unconscious in the intensive care unit of the local hospital, we reorganised some of the stuff just so that I had somewhere to sleep and tried to create some sort of sense out of the remainder. We felt like traitors and we would have given anything for him to wake up and tell us to stop interfering and that no reasonable person needed more than six inches of horizontal surface visible at any given time.

He died without knowing that we'd started organising the mess and boxing up things for charity or to put into storage. Ruefully we laughed when we found half a five pound note in between two dusty books, saying it was our fitting inheritance.

We never did find the other half. A little under a year later, my mother moved out of the bungalow to be near me and this time, the decluttering, which had been slowly progressing for nine months, had to be finished in the space of two weeks. There would be no room in the flat at the sheltered complex.

That was in 2013 and I still feel scarred by the experience of disposing of so much one way or another. My mother's flat is now tidy in an untidy sort of way and most of the retained boxes of stuff are in our garage, although periodically she kidnaps one to rummage through. She misses the clutter of fifty-one years of marriage to a hoarder. Actually, if truth be told, she thinks the kidnapping has been done by me and that I am keeping them out of reach in the rafters of the garage just to annoy her.

In the process of helping her move from bungalow to flat, I unearthed a tin (yes a tin) of furniture polish from the kitchen and said to my mother, 'er… isn't this the same tin you had when I was a little girl?'

'Probably,' she said, 'the thing is,' she added with much wisdom, 'there's always something more interesting to do than housework.'

Dad and Mum and Julia and Me

I published this book as an 80th birthday present for my mother
Christine.

My mother's parents moved down from Scotland in the
1930s. Mum was born in Twickenham and grew up in Hampton.

Dad meanwhile, with ancestors from Kent, Ireland, possibly
Scandanavia and definitely what is now Ukraine, was born in
Ilford and grew up in Cranford. One of Dad's grandfathers was
Frederick Hitchin-Kemp, author of 'A general history of the
Kemp and Kempe families of Great Britain and her colonies' and
one of his great-grandfathers was Hermann Liebstein, author of
'Notes of Expository Addresses on the Book of Revelation'. The
Kemp book really does include reference to an ancestor fishing a
whale out of the Thames sometime in the middle ages. The
chances of Dad not becoming a story-lover and writer was nil.

Mum met Dad on a photography course at Richmond
College. She left home to marry Dad in 1961 and when he died,
fifty-one years later, it was the first time she had lived or managed
on her own. I am full of admiration at her courage to up-sticks,
move near to me and start joining things. She tackles banking, the
internet and Photoshop with stubborn determination and a quiet
fire.

This book, as you may have gathered, is not exactly a
memoir. Some of it is true, some of it is sort of true, some real
events that happened at different times have been put together to
make a narrative. All of the 'Dad Dreams' stories are of course,
completely fictional but this was only due to lack of opportunity,
I'm sure.

Dad was a prolific writer and I have boxes of his typed
manuscripts and a few digital files which I hope to publish one
day including 'The Adventures of Myfanwy Price'. I only have
the first story and the Boanerges typescript with his drawing is on
the next page.

He preferred writing science fiction. One day I asked him why he didn't write something about real life and he said real life was rather dull and went on: '*you* try to write an interesting story about two pensioners and a mobility scooter'. I said 'OK then'. The result was 'Coffee at Tiffany's' and this story was probably one of the exercises which got me back into writing after several years in a creative wilderness.

Shortly after that, I was rushing to a meeting in London. The weather was dreadful. As I ran along Westminster Bridge in freezing rain, I saw two people (one in an electric wheelchair) and what appeared to be a cat in a basket. I texted Dad and challenged him to explain why they were there. He said 'all right but you do it too.' My suggestion was 'Ellie is a Cat' which is now 'Cumulatorus Confundendum'.

I started 'The Test Drive' as a birthday present present in 2012, but as the year progressed, Dad's chronic illness worsened and he was admitted to Singleton Hospital. I became too anxious and sad and tired with travelling to finish it, but thought maybe I would manage to do so by Father's Day, which would be on 17th June. I travelled up to visit Dad in hospital on Saturday 9th June. We chatted alone for a long time. He was quiet and serious, worried about Mum and very tired. On the night of Sunday 10th June he had a cardiac arrest and was taken to Morriston Hospital to be put on life support.

So I really did rush across from London on a wet, cold June day and my sister Julia really did leave her son in Leicester to rush down to join us. Yet however unhappy, the week when Dad was in intensive care was also very special. It was probably the first time Mum, Julia and I had ever been together, just the three of us, as adults, for more than a day or so. We cried, we laughed, we remembered, we tidied. Dad died two days before Father's Day.

But this book isn't meant to be sad, nor is it meant to be a warts-and-all memoir. Dad wasn't faultless, but then nor am I. We argued and bickered like most fathers and daughters. Perhaps being the eldest, I had to do more arguing and bickering than

Julia. Perhaps she was just better at appearing to go with the flow but actually doing her own thing (she still is). Sometimes, in later years, it seemed as if Dad and I got on best by text.

But he was a man with a heart of gold. If anyone 'entertained angels unawares' it was Dad. He was a kind and faithful friend, 'adopting' strangers in a strange land as additional adult daughters: Lei-Nah Lee and Ana Sena and also Mum's South African cousin's daughter, Claudia Meyer.

Lei-Nah sadly died some years before Dad. Ana and Claudia still miss him desperately.

In this book, I purposely stuck with childhood memories because that was when Dad was still perfect. I wasn't a teenager trying to get to the phone before he realised the caller was a boy; I wasn't a young woman trying to explain why I didn't need to be home at eleven if I didn't want to; I wasn't an older woman wondering whether he would ever stop embarrassing me (answer: never). When I was little, Dad knew everything. I wasn't too happy that people said I looked like him (he was plump and balding) but I did want to be like him. Apart from when he had shocking headaches caused by a serious car accident, he was happy, care-free. He didn't mind about mess. There was always a new hobby on the go. He read aloud with a myriad voices, enthralling us, drawing us into fantastic worlds with dragons and elves or martians and robots. He was undaunted.

I wish Dad was still alive so that he could read what I've written. I wish I could show him how to self-publish his own work if he chose. I wish he was still texting me even though the texts were a thousand characters long. I wish we could still argue. I wish I could serve him roast duck and peas once more.

On the other hand, I don't wish I could dance with him again, because last time I did that I ended up with a bruised foot.

Apart from half of half a fiver and boxes of writing, Dad's real legacy to me was love. Julia and I never felt less than completely loved and accepted. Our triumphs were our parent's triumphs, our disappointments were theirs too.

I loved my father very much. I miss him. I love and admire
my mother hugely. She had never lived alone until he died and I
know that he worried about leaving her to cope. But cope she has,
moving to leave near me and making friends in a new place. She
has mastered a new computer, perfecting her Photoshop skills and
woe betide the printer which won't do her bidding. I hope this
book will make her laugh and remind her of happy times that
were and might have been. And I hope that she and Julia feel this
is a true reflection of the mad, messy, kind, infuriating, creative,
faithful man who was my father, Richard Downes.

the Scruffiest Eagle she had ever seen landed on the
brach beside her.

    " Have you got anything to keep my feathers tidy,
Miss Price," said the Eagle.

    Mis Myfannwy Price was very frightened. She had
heard that Eagles ate Squirrels, and this one was

Glossary

In case any words or phrases are unfamiliar.

Bungalow: a one storey house.

Caravan: in this case a touring caravan or trailer.

Ice-lolly: a lolly is short for 'lollipop' which is a hard sweet (candy) on a stick; an ice-lolly is a 'popsickle'.

Keep shtum: silent, under wraps. It's Yiddish but is common slang in the UK

Semi-detached house: one of two houses which are joined along one wall as opposed to a detached house which stands alone or a terrace, where several are joined together.

Toddler: a child who's toddling. E.g. 12 months to 2 years or thereabouts.

Water-boatmen: properly called Corixidae. It's a kind of insect which appears to skate across the surface of water.

Welsh Bible: Wales is a separate country within the UK in the same way as Scotland and Northern Ireland are. Modern Welsh has its roots in the ancient language which the British would have spoken before the Anglo Saxon invasion. The Bretons in Northern France were originally refugees from that invasion, crossing the channel from southern Britain - hence the name Brittany (little Britain as opposed to Great Britain). Breton, Welsh and Cornish are very similar. There was a major Christian revival in Wales in 1904 and huge great family bibles in Welsh were often to be found in older houses (we could only assume the previous owners hadn't wanted theirs and so left it behind). NB if you've read this far without falling asleep, interesting fact: there is a community in Patagonia which was made up of Welsh settlers who went there in 1865. Welsh is still spoken there along side Spanish.

5p piece: a small coin worth five pence. There are one hundred pence in one pound. Prior to decimalisation in 1971, there were two hundred and forty pence in one pound and coins included halfpennies (ha'pennies), threepenny pieces (thru'penny bits), sixpences (tanners), one shilling pieces (worth twelve pence and known as bobs); two shilling pieces (florins). After decimalisation, old sixpences, shillings and florins were kept in circulation for several years and were equivalent to 2½p, 5p and 10p respectively. A sixpence was a small coin and was often given as pocket money or a small gift. After several years, the new ½p coin was withdrawn and the old sixpences, shillings and florins went out of circulation. 5p and 10p pieces got smaller and the current (2017) 5p piece is roughly the size of an old sixpence and slightly smaller than a US 5c piece.

Dedication

This book is dedicated to my brave and lovely mother Christine Downes for her 80th birthday and to Julia Smith who will still be my naughty little sister when we're mad old ladies.

In memory of my lovely, exasperating, creative father Richard Downes (January 1938 - June 2012).

Acknowledgments

All internal illustrations are by Paula Harmon except the picture of Myfanwy Price which is by Richard Downes

I hope you enjoyed this book.

With many thanks to Julie Eger and Val Portelli, my reviewers, for their input and support.

Also many thanks to my daughter Zoe, for being the model (by way of photographs of her as a child) for many of the sketches.

Acknowledging the use of the titles of 'I'm Walking Backwards for Christmas' by Spike Milligan; 'Bat Out of Hell' by Jim Steinman; 'Magical Mystery Tour' by Lennon McCartney; 'Donald Where's Your Troosers' by Andy Stewart; 'Bless Your Beautiful Hide' by Mercer, Kasha, Hirschhorn; 'Climb Every Mountain' by Oscar Hammerstein II.

About Paula Harmon

Paula Harmon was born in North London but her father relocated the family every two years until they settled in South Wales when Paula was eight. She graduated from Chichester University before making her home in Gloucestershire and then Dorset where she has lived since 2005. She is a civil servant, married with two children at university.

https://paulaharmondownes.wordpress.com
https://twitter.com/Paula_S_Harmon
https://www.facebook.com/pg/paulaharmonwrites

Books available from: http://viewauthor.at/PHAuthorpage

Murder Britannica

It's AD 190 in Southern Britain. Lucretia won't let her get-rich-quick scheme be undermined by minor things like her husband's death. But a gruesome discovery leads wise-woman Tryssa to start asking awkward questions.

Murder Durnovaria

It's AD 191. Lucretia last saw Durnovaria as a teenager. Now she's back to claim an inheritance. Who could imagine an old ring bought in the forum could bring lead to Tryssa having to help local magistrate Amicus discover who would rather kill than reveal long-buried truths.

The Cluttering Discombobulator

The story of one man's battle against common sense and the family caught up in the chaos around him.

Kindling

Secrets and mysteries, strangers and friends. Stories as varied and changing as British skies.

The Advent Calendar

Christmas without the hype - stories for midwinter.

<u>The Case of the Black Tulips</u> (first in the 'Caster & Fleet Mysteries) (with Liz Hedgecock)
When Katherine Demeray opens a letter, little does she imagine it will lead her to join forces with socialite Connie Swift, racing against time to solve mysteries and right wrongs.

<u>Weird and Peculiar Tales</u> (with Val Portelli)
Short stories from this world and beyond.

The Quest
In a parallel universe, dragons are used for fuel and the people who understand them are feared as spies and traitors.

The Seaside Dragon (a book for children)
Laura and Jane expect a weekend break without wifi. They don't expect to have to rescue their parents from terrible danger.

Ingram Content Group UK Ltd.
Milton Keynes UK
UKHW021946040723
424555UK00014B/1549